A Red River Romance

Book two

Praying my story gives God glory!

All of Caryl's Books

Historical Christian Texas Romances
Vow Unbroken
Hearts Stolen
Hope Reborn

Contemporary Christian
Red River Romances
The Preacher's Faith
Sing a New Song
Apple Orchard Romances
Lady Luck's a Loser

Biblical fiction
The Generations
A Little Lower Than the Angels
Then the Deluge Comes

Mid-Grade
River Bottom Ranch Stories
The Adventures of Sergeant Socks
The Journey Home
The Bravest heart
Amazing Graci, Guardian of Goats

Miscellaneous Novels
The Thief of Dreams (PG-17, written for secular readers)
The Price Paid (WWII military novel based on true experiences)
Absolute Pi (audio)
Apple Orchard B&B (re-released as Lady Luck's a Loser)

Non-fiction
Great Firehouse Cooks of Texas
Antiquing in North Texas

Five-Star Reviews for
Sing a New Song ♫♪*•♪

Sing A New Song is a delightful breath of Christian air. McAdoo writes in such an eloquent way bringing her audience always nearer to God. She opens her readers' minds to fresh ways of viewing Christian life and all it has to offer.

The characters are loveable and react to one another in humorous ways. The romantic tale is just as lovely as always demonstrating Christian virtues we all be best to remember. The story was illuminating in how it shares the Gospel in such a beautiful way.

The words from Samuel's sermons as well as the gorgeous lyrics of Mary Esther's songs fill our hearts with newfound worship for Our Lord. Truly an inspiring tale. It is Christian fiction in its best; recounting a romantic love story while bringing its readers closer to God. A treasure for sure.

--Christine Barber, Canadian author of Broken to Pieces

Disappointed by love, but still saving herself for "Mr. Right", Mary Esther returns to her hometown of Clarksville, Texas and reunites with her best childhood friend, Samuel—the boy who stole her first kiss at the age of twelve and a descendant and namesake of Levi Baylor from Caryl's previous historical novel series which I just enjoy so much. You won't want to miss this modern day romance! I couldn't put it down! Loved it!

--Louise Koiner, avid reader, Clarksville, Texas

Excited

I'm just so excited
'bout what the Lord is doing!
I'm just so excited
of what I know He will do!
I'm just so excited,
and He is delighted
with my anticipation
of what He's going to do!

2nd verse
I get to be a part
of what the Lord is doing!
I get to be a part
of what I know He will do!
I get to be a part,
and He's got a good plan,
He's called me for His purpose,
I have a role to play!

And I'm just so excited…
Repeat and repeat and repeat

Sing a New Song

✝ ♥ ♫♪ •*•♪♫ ✝

✝ ♥ ♫♪ •*•♪♫ ✝

Caryl McAdoo

First Edition

April 2015

Printed and bound in the United States of America

ISBN-13 978-1508-7423-2-6
ISBN-10   1508742324

Inquiries for volume purchases of this book may be directed to
Post Office Box 622, Clarksville, Texas 75426

♪♪*•♪ Dedication

My hope is built on nothing less than Jesus and His righteousness; I dare not trust the sweet refrain, but wholly lean on Jesus name. I pray my story gives God glory, and so I dedicate Sing a New Song to Him and His Kingdom.

There would be no stories, there would be no songs without Him loving me so much that He gives them to me. He is my everything. His love overwhelms me. How can it be so great?

The biggest blessing He's blessed my life with if my Ron, my husband of almost 47 years, my best friend, my protector, greatest cheerleader, supporter and encourager. I always said if I could change one thing about this near-perfect man, it would be to make him a singer, a lover of music ☺

He is the song in my heart and the love of my life, but is tone deaf! But nothing is too hard for God. And so I wait with expectation.

And for my friends in Clarksville and Red River County, Texas...I'm so grateful the Lord brought us north and east. I love this area with all its rich history and quaint country living. I love almost everything about it and can hardly wait to see what God has in store!

Though I'll probably always be counted a 'newcomer' here, I'm blessed to call Clarksville and Red River County home. This series is for all of you!

One of Caryl's New Songs ♫♪*•♪

Amazing

It isn't only Your grace that's amazing!
The sound is as sweet of Your faithfulness, too.
You never slumber or sleep.
You've promised my soul to keep,
And when I get in too deep,
Your love always lifts me.

Chorus
Amazing! You're so amazing!
Everything about You, everything that You do:
The stars in the sky
A baby's first cry
The newness of Spring
And the joy that it brings!
You're so amazing, Lord!
You're amazing to me!

Your blood is amazing!
There's so much power in the Blood!
You lovingkindness amazes me, too;
It's fresh each morn.
Your sacrifice is amazing!
You paid the price
To set me free!

Chorus

Acknowledgements ✝ ♥ ♫♪

How can I say thanks? Even though I am a 'wordsmith' (one who takes words and heats them and beats them into the lyrical phrases that please readers' ears, I fall woefully short of adequate thanks to my Creator and the Lover of my soul. Before Him, an unworthy sinner bound for hell. After Him, covered in the Blood of the Lamb, I'm special, a daughter of the King, righteous and useful in His service.

So grateful for the new songs He gives me, I love praising and worshipping His Holy name! The Great I Am keeps me singing as I go!

I love the Dedication and Acknowledgement pages because I get to brag on Abba and my favorite people. At the top of that list is Ron. He's such a great writer himself and the reason I have such awesome heroes. He keeps me singing, too (but he did ban show tunes ☺).

Grateful for so many friends and helpers who so bless me over and again, I find words insufficient to tell how much. Instead, I'd love to hug each one tight—counting at least to twenty—to show them. After all, writers are supposed to SHOW not TELL.

Lenda Selph is my Heaven-sent proofer and official comma-kazi queen, and along with the sharp, fresh eyes of Louise Koiner, Joy Gibson, Christine Barber, Cass Wessel, and Leah Jones, help me make sure all my oversights get corrected. And my eVALUaters and friends who share posts and review my novels at Amazon and Goodreads, or click 'Like' on Facebook, Tweets, and recommend my books to their friends. I need y'all and thank y'all and know God will bless you for blessing me! My cup literally overflows!

Thank you. I just have to shout it! THANK YOU! ☺

I love to sing Your praise, Lord! My favorite place to be is bowed before Your throne!

... Caryl ♥ ♫♪ ♱ ♥ ♫

It is a good thing to give thanks unto the LORD, and to sing praises unto thy name, O Most High: Psalm 92:1

Hear, O ye kings; give ear, O ye princes; I, even I, will sing unto the LORD; I will sing praise to the LORD God of Israel. Judges 5:3

Saying, I will declare thy name unto my brethren, in the midst of the church will I sing praise unto thee. Hebrews 2:12

Therefore I will give thanks unto thee, O LORD, among the heathen, and I will sing praises unto thy name. 2 Samuel 22:50

I will be glad and rejoice in thee: I will sing praise to thy name, O thou most High. Psalm 9:2

To the end that my glory may sing praise to thee, and not be silent. O LORD my God, I will give thanks unto thee for ever. Psalm 30:12

While I live will I praise the LORD: I will sing praises unto my God while I have any being. Psalm 146:2

✝♥♫ Chapter One

Mary Esther waved her key card then turned around and extended her hand. He took it and pulled her toward him, leaned in. The desire to close her eyes and surrender, let him kiss her, washed over like a sweet spring shower.

She should pull away, but instead, at the last heartbeat, turned her cheek instead.

He smelled of summer pomegranates carried on ocean breezes, crisp and clean, though he'd been on the go with her all day. His lips brushed her burning skin. He kissed her then moved on to her ear. "I don't want to leave. Can I come in?"

She pressed her fingertips on his chest, pushing a bit, and smiled. "No, you may not. But you can write me. I love long letters."

"How about I call instead? Where's the band headed next?"

"Atlanta."

He nodded then seemed to study her shoes a moment. When he looked back up, a troubled expression wrinkled his forehead. Staring into her eyes, he reached up and tapped the tip of her nose.

"There's something I need to tell you before you go."

"Okay. What is it?"

"I'm, uh…" He grimaced, showing his perfect teeth clenched, then offered her a weak smile. "See? Uh, I'm married. Well..." He sighed. "Separated; I mean she's gone, left me. No one's –"

"You're married?"

"Legally, yes—for now—and you're beautiful."

She pushed him back, hard. The urge to slap his face burned her hand as though she had, but a long time ago, she learned not to go around hitting guys.

"Married? What was the last week all about, you jerk? Get away from me, Richard. Go home. I cannot believe you…you …you're nothing but a.…" The only words that came to mind weren't worth speaking.

"Mary Esther, I…"

She shook her head to make them go away. "Mercy, man, you're an associate pastor. And you'd be an adulterer, too?"

He recoiled, as though the reality of how he'd been acting the last week cut him just as the cock's crows had cut Peter. A horror filled his eyes. He shook his head no and opened his mouth, but no words came out.

Backing a step, he turned then hurried down the hotel's hall, throwing a lame, "Sorry, I.…" over his shoulder.

"Dear Lord, my God. How could I have thought he might be the one? The one I've been looking for, praying for?" Her heart pounded. The desire to run after him and slap some smarts into him faded.

He turned the corner; she pushed her door open, stepped inside, then hugged it, resting her forehead on its edge. It hit her. If that guy wasn't the one, maybe there wasn't a man out there for her. It seemed no one ever saw the real her.

Oh, they loved her voice, her songs, or the way she sang. Who knew? Maybe the way she looked, or walked, or blah blah blah.

She shut the door and flung herself across the bed. It wasn't fair. Tears welled and overflowed, wetting the white duvet. She grabbed the towel she'd wrapped her wet hair in that morning and pulled it under her face.

Wouldn't do to get mascara all over the cover. The tears kept coming with no end in sight and the enormity of what she'd been thinking. That such an idiot could have been husband material!

How could she? Didn't she have any discernment at all?

Was she so caught up in romance and concerned she'd never find Mister Right that she lost sight of character? Hadn't she prayed? She searched her memory, but it didn't register that she ever asked God if Richard was the one.

Married, indeed!

She screamed into the towel, bawling like an idiot. Why, why, why couldn't she see it? She flipped to her back and stared, suddenly silent, at the ceiling. The stillness rang in her ears. Her breath caught. She swallowed.

Then it hit her, she wasn't in love with the man. She barely knew him. The inference she'd never know love is what broke her heart. What caused all the tears.

But didn't God promise the desires of her heart?

She loved the idea of love, of belonging to one man, sharing his life… children. If that was not to be, what had she saved herself for? Wait a minute. That wasn't the Lord. She saved herself in obedience to God.

If she never found a man, if God never sent a Mister Right into her life, she would still remain chaste. For Him, no one else.

The least she could do after what He had done for her.

Besides His sweet salvation, He'd given her music, new songs, and a decent voice. As long as she could offer praise and worship, extol His Holy name, as long as He invited her into His throne room….

Sleep finally found her, and then she was twelve again.

She stared at his casket, hated that they kept it closed, but understood the decision. Mama explained that he'd been mangled so badly. She wiped her cheeks. Praise God, at least he was in Heaven.

"Someday, Daddy, we'll all be together again." A hand slipped over hers. She looked down, studied the stubby fingers intertwining with her own, then followed the arm up to Samuel Baylor's face.

Her best friend since first grade kept a solemn expression and squeezed her hand. With the whites of his eyes red streaked and his cheeks wet, he nodded south. "Com'ere, I want to show you something."

She looked back to the casket then found her mother, safe in the center of a sea of black dresses and suits. He pulled, and she went along, joined him to see whatever he wanted her to. "I didn't know you were here."

"I loved your dad. I would have walked all the way from English if I had to, but…" He grinned. "PawPaw let me take his truck."

"Really? All the way from English?"

"Yep, but he made me promise to stay on the back roads."

"Samuel, what if you'd had a wreck?"

He waved her off. "I've been driving all over the farm forever. Roads are easier."

"No, not since forever. You told me he let you drive the first time on your tenth birthday."

"Well, two years is like forever." He stopped and pointed at a weathered headstone. "Here, look at this."

She studied the marker. "The Levi Bartholomew Baylor, right? Born November 12, 1817; Traveled home December 11, 1881. He was sixty-four when he passed. Beloved husband to Rosaleen, Faithful father to Charlie, Bart, Austin, Daniel, Rusk, and Rachel Rose."

"Yes, ma'am. My great, great, great grandfather—or maybe four greats. I'm not sure. Anyway, did you know he was one of the first Texas Rangers?"

"Yes, Samuel Levi Baylor, you've told me all about him, more'n once."

"Oh, right, I remember. Come over here." He tugged on her hand, led her around a big oak then stopped in front of another old grave.

She stopped then studied on that one. "Peter Passamor, doctor. Do you know him or something?"

A blur came at her, then his lips pressed against hers. Right there in front of God and all her family, at her daddy's funeral, he was kissing her. For a heartbeat, she kissed him back, then jerked away and swung hard.

Her open hand connected square on his cheek. Seemed to shock him almost as much as her. Hopefully, it hurt his face more than her palm. She never expected it to sting her hand so badly, but he deserved it.

Shouldn't be stealing a kiss, wasn't right.

She jerked upright in bed. The dream lingered, hadn't ever taken such a turn before; before it always focused on the loss of her father, not her friend. She woke with no tears this time and minus the usual heartache of her daddy dying so young.

Instead, the night vision left her a crystal clear realization: exactly what she needed to do. She rolled out of bed and filled the too-little coffee pot with water from the mini-sink's faucet.

A shower didn't change her mind, nor did packing or a trip downstairs for breakfast. Her resolve flickered a bit as she stood in front of the door across the hall from her room. She smiled.

"Well, my bags are packed, and I am ready to go. Indeed, I am standing here outside their door, and I really do hate to wake them up to say goodbye."

She rapped one knuckle three times. "I am not leaving on a jet plane, though, and I need my money." Her mind made up, she tapped twice more on the door. Shortly, it cracked open. Her friend's face appeared.

"Morning, Mare." She glanced at the suitcases. "You packed already? Thought we weren't pulling out 'til after lunch."

"Yes, that's correct, well, for y'all. Brad in there? I need to talk with him."

"Sure, give us a second." The door closed then after better than sixty of the requested ticks of the clock, the portal swung open. "Come on in."

The mess startled her, but oh well, not everyone had been raised by a mother and grandmother who were bona fide clean freaks.

The guitar man finger-combed his hair. "Hey, how's our song bird this fine morning? Have a sit down. Got us that new tune you've been working on?"

She emptied one of two clothes-covered chairs at the small table, dumping its contents onto the floor. "I'm fine, and no. This won't take long. How'd you know I was working on a song?"

"Aren't you always?" He waved her off. "What can we do for you?"

"I'm going home. Sorry, but I need to. I'd like whatever money I've got coming."

"Home? No way, Mary Esther. We're booked in Atlanta, bus leaves at one."

"I know, and I hear you, Brad, but I am going home."

"Dallas or Denver?"

"Neither. Going all the way home. To Clarksville."

Bev twisted her hair up and clipped it on top of her head. "Why, Mare, what's wrong?"

"Nothing, everything. I came to the realization this morning. I need a break. Being on the road… It isn't… Let's just say it isn't what I expected."

"But –"

"No. I've got to go, and I'm leaving. Now. This morning. You know all the songs as well as me, Bev. Take the lead." She faced Brad. "She can do it. Let's talk dollars. Where do we stand?"

The band's leader alternated between bullying and begging, but in the end handed over fifteen hundred cash with a promise of full accounting from his CPA for the last eighteen months. She'd been singing and writing songs for the band.

Hopefully, he'd be a man of his word.

"Is this all over Rich being married?"

"You knew?" She looked from Brad to his wife. He stared back, but Bev averted her eyes. How could they not tell her?

"He's a friend; you two made a cute couple."

She glared at him. "You're worse than that idiot. Why in the world didn't you tell me, or better still, tell him to leave me alone?" She faced Bev. "And you? You knew, too?"

"He's getting a divorce."

Mary Esther backed toward the door. "Whatever." She put her hand on the knob then all the good times, all the folks who'd been moved by their music flooded her soul. "God bless you guys, and please do have the accountant contact me."

"I will, God bless you, too."

✝♥♫♪ •*•♪♫✝

Five hundred and seven miles south and west, Samuel Levi Baylor woke seven mornings later having dreamed about the same horrible day as Mary Esther had the week before. He rubbed his cheek. Still stung after twenty years.

The handprint had long vanished, but not the aching in his heart. He hadn't even got to tell her goodbye. Her mother left that same afternoon for Big D.

He showered, shaved, and geared up.

Bless the Lord, his last day at the Cross Arrow. He loved working cows, but stringing hot wire did not ring his bell. Too much like work. His dad always said work was work, but far as Samuel figured, not a reason in the world it couldn't or shouldn't be fun, too.

Lord knew he needed the money.

Well, some might argue buying that registered Angus bull he wanted couldn't be classified as a need. Sure would improve his herd though.

He took care of all his chores and still beat everyone to the bottoms along Langford Creek. Though he understood the purpose of putting farmland behind the electric fence, sure couldn't understand farming prime pastureland.

To his way of thinking, sod busting proved the bigger gamble over breeding prime stock. He'd seen it way more than once. Some new guy buying up a big block of Red River County, thinking he knew how to bring in a harvest.

A few actually succeeded turning a profit; the majority cashed in on their insurance. What always got him, they kept coming down here thinking they could do it like they did up north; much wiser to follow the locals' leads.

He chuckled at the memory of that one guy who thought he could make no-till work on the prairie's black dirt.

Finally, the foreman backed everyone up then flipped on the solar charger. For half a heartbeat, it seemed stuck then the needle jumped all the way to the green.

"Looks like we're good to go, boys. That does it for this section." He nodded toward the hill where the headquarters sat nestled between the two giant feed silos and the oversized hay barns.

Words of approval mixed with a bit of rabblerousing worked its way around. Hats were removed then settled back, brows mopped.

"Come get your money then, hombres." The man looked at Samuel. "You Bible thumpers can come on, too."

He ignored the jab. He'd been knowing the old cowboy for years, and truth be told, the man professed to be a Christian himself, but of the more sedate variety.

Once he collected his wages, with a promise of a call when the dozer man had the next block ready, he marched to his grandfather's old truck. Guess it belonged to him now, since PawPaw passed, but Samuel couldn't....

Never got in it without thinking of him.

Then like he'd gone brain dead, he turned left instead of going the long way. Oh well, turning around would be too much trouble, so he kept going. Mercy, he'd just dreamed about her.

Going by her old house shouldn't trigger another nightmare. Either way, he had the salve that could soothe his soul.

♱ ♥ ♫♪ •*•♪♫ ♱

Mary Esther fished in the bottom of her heavy purse looking for the house key. She balanced the bag on her knee, hopping once to keep her balance. The old door opened with the first bit of weight against it. She stepped inside.

Instead of her mother standing over the stove and her dad sitting in his chair, only cobwebs greeted her. It smelled musty. An old wooden chair with a blue vinyl padded seat and a strip across the back brought a smile.

She remembered when her father brought that dining set home from the Goodwill store in Paris. She couldn't have been more than seven or eight then. Why did that one get left? She liked those chairs.

But then her grandmother had all her own furniture. Mary Esther didn't even get to have her own bed go to Dallas with her.

Took her weeks to get used to that hard one she slept on at Mimi Lady's.

She poked and prodded the old farmhouse she'd grown up in. It seemed sound enough, but a hole in the floor of her parents' old room took her back. A rabbit scurried past in its escape.

"Oh, Lord, am I crazy for even thinking what I'm thinking?"

Before any answer came from above or her heart, the deep-throated rumble of an old truck drew her around, then tires crushing gravel quickened her pulse. She ran to the kitchen and split the old blinds' slats.

A faded blue truck filled the drive just beyond the carport. She knew that old truck. No. It couldn't be. Twenty years ago—had it been that long?—No…please, God, don't let it be so.

The front door banged against the living room wall. Daddy never did replace that stopper. "Hello? Whoever you are, you're trespassing here." The male voice sounded somewhat familiar, but surely PawPaw wasn't still alive. Could he be?

She started trying to do the math in her head, but that was useless. She marched around to the breezeway between the kitchen and living room. The interloper headed down the hall toward the back.

"Pray tell, how does one trespass her own property?"

The guy turned toward her and stared. "Mary Esther? Is that you? Really you?" A big old grin almost cracked his face right in two.

The twelve-year-old boy who drove that same truck to her daddy's funeral stood over six feet tall, a full grown man decked out in jeans, blue long-sleeved work shirt, and scuffed boots, but she'd know him anywhere.

He gawked. "It is, isn't it?"

"Yes, it's me. How in the world have you been, Samuel? How'd you know I was in town?"

"Well, I'll be. Blessed. I've been blessed, but I didn't have any idea. None. What are you doing here? Slumming?"

She refused to take the bait. "I'll have you to know I'm moving back. Just now I was trying decide if the old girl is worth fixing up."

"Really? What? You're not singing anymore?"

"Of course, I am. No way will I ever stop singing, you goof, but I can sing in Clarksville same as in Dallas. I quit the band though. I'm sick of the road. If you could call it that."

He nodded and looked around. "So what do you think?"

That he didn't offer to give her a hello hug was just wrong, but she didn't say anything about it. "I don't know, but what about you? Are you married? How's your grandfather? Y'all still living in English?"

He laughed a melodious bass that begged for a harmony. The boy's promise had bloomed.

"Same old girl, except you got famous."

"Oh, not so much."

"PawPaw—thanks for asking—went home three years ago, and no, I haven't found a lady who would have me, and yes, I'm still in English. I've doubled its size though, got me a right nice block of black land."

"What are you doing? Farming?"

"Heavens no. Still trying to make a cowboy."

She nodded. The old timers and cow punchers all told the same story. Not a one of them ever made it, but they were all still trying.

"Okay, now that we've caught up, what do you think about my house? Is she worth moving? I was thinking of setting her back in the woods a bit, in front of that deep pool daddy dug. You remember it? Should I bulldoze her or find me a carpenter and fix her up?"

"Of course I remember that pool, and you have found your carpenter. Me. If you want, I'll have a look see."

She studied him as he inspected her childhood home, in and around, up in the attic then even under. "Some damage, but not too bad. Nice-sized beehive in the northeast corner of the attic, but we can smoke them out, no problem."

"Think she'd hold together getting moved…? Is she worth the effort?"

"The house is sound. Shouldn't give you any trouble. You serious about needing help?"

"I sure am, definitely. Want the job?" She grinned and was a twelve-year-old again. "But don't smoke out those bees. Let's find someone to move 'em, I've always wanted a hive."

"Know just the man, librarian's husband."

Chapter Two ✞♥♫♪

Why was she doing this? Had his first love blown into town with a wild hare to fix up the old place and then she'd be gone again? Samuel shrugged. What did he have to lose? "Am I doing it by myself, or can I get some more hands in here?"

"What do you need?"

"Labor for sure. I don't know yet, I'll need to move her first. The rest depends on how much remodel you want. I can give you a better idea then. I can do most of it myself, but if you're after speed, I'll need a crew."

"What kind of labor?"

"Someone who can swing a sledge, a shagger –"

"Excuse me?"

"Someone to haul whatever needs to be lugged around."

"Oh. What else to get started?"

"Guess we need to talk money, carpentry pays more than ranch day work."

"Oh, I fully suspected it would."

For the next few minutes, she sparred with him over how much and exactly when he'd collect his pay, almost like being ten again and playing monopoly with her and her mother. He'd always give her the best side of the negotiations—well, after she insisted.

He couldn't remember a more fun time. Those three weeks he spent at her house…the best ever.

She stuck her hand out. "Deal then?" Then sucked it back. "Oh wait, you added found. What is that exactly?"

"That means you bring dinner. Old time ranch hand talk."

"Okay." Grinning, she reached back out toward him. "Deal?"

He studied her fingers, a third again longer than he remembered but just as lovely, long and slender with painted nails. Sure hoped he wasn't making a big mistake. "What about my labor?"

"You're looking at her."

"You're not serious?"

"Well, sure I am. The more I can do, the less it'll cost me."

"You do have enough money, right?"

"I've got a dab, been saving for a while. Plus there's more on the way if the accountants play fair."

He stuck his hand out and grasped hers. Sparks raced from her palm all the way to his heart, as though nothing had changed, but she didn't seem to feel a thing. How could she still do that to him after so long a time?

"Deal, but promise me if the dollars run low, I get notice. A week would be nice."

"Of course, when can you start?"

"Tomorrow soon enough?" He kept hold of her hand and gave a slight compulsory shake at every question.

A tsunami washed over him, the urge to kiss those lips. But he'd been there and wanted no part of getting slapped again, or worse, her running away from him again.

"Yes, sir, what time?"

"I've got chores first thing every morning. How does six-thirty sound?"

"Like the middle of the night, but I can be here."

"Where you bunkin'?"

"The Old Courthouse B & B. What do you want for lunch?"

"I don't care, but here in the valley, the noon meal is still called dinner."

"Right, I've been gone too long."

"Yes, you have."

He released her hand, even though he didn't want to. Holding on any longer would have been weird. Did he detect a hint of something or was it only because he wanted to? Probably not, though.

Why would a big time Christian singer be interested in a nobody country cowboy she used to know?

Besides, now she was his boss, not that she hadn't always been the boss of him.

✞ ♥ ♫♪ •*•♪♫ ✞

Mary Esther watched him drive away. Mercy, Lord, why was he acting like that? Did he hate her? And that nasty remark about slumming. Why would he say such a thing? What could that be all about?

Her hand—the one he'd held—of its own accord rose to her nose, and she inhaled. She'd forgotten how good he smelled.

And six-thirty? She couldn't remember the last time she'd been up at six-thirty ante meridian. Had the man turned into some kind of sadist? Why didn't she tell him no way? They could start at nine just as easy—what was she thinking?

Or at least eight-thirty, any more reasonable, civilized time of the morning suited her better.

Meant getting up at four, ugh. Well, he could forget her doing anything but the basics. She chuckled to herself.

Wasn't like he didn't know what she looked like in the mornings. What a deal her dad and Samuel's grandfather worked out, her best friend staying with them while they teamed a load to Alaska.

Best three weeks ever. He did her chores, all she had to do was tag along for the fun of it. He'd start all kind of games to play, even with her mother. While he hated staying in her pinkie pink room, she got to sleep with Mama and they'd talked late into the nights.

Mary Esther wandered back to her old doorway. The walls still wore her preteen passion for magenta. She smiled, reminiscing, and stepped on down the hall to her parents' room. Oh, Lord, how she still missed him.

Why did he have to leave so early? His death changed her life so much. He would never have let Mom haul her off to Irving. Had she stayed put, would she have a house full of babies by now?

Yeah, right, and be miserable dreaming about a life on the road? She retreated to her car, took one last look at the old place, then headed to town. Turning at the square, she wove her way to the Old Courthouse B&B, her temporary home.

Once she and Samuel got the old girl livable, that would save her a chunk, even with getting the monthly, no breakfast rate.

The next morning—or rather in the middle of the night—when her alarm clock so rudely interrupted her deep sleep, she slapped at it, rolled over, and snuggled down. But in no time the loud devil squawked again.

Barely crawling out of bed, she leaned toward the offensive machine and squinted to focus on the angry red numbers glaring at her: five-fifty-five. What? Three fives, God's number for grace.

She ran her fingers through her hair and headed left, stopped, then went right. What should she do first? She glanced again at the beast. Four minutes until six! Oh good grief, she'd never make it on time.

Out the window, where the light from the yet-to-rise sun brightened the night, the new day pressed to be dawned.

She hated being up before the sun.

Like being a kid again, getting ready for school, but back then, her mother and grandmother made sure she went to bed earlier and turned the lights out and lay there in the dark counting sheep. Oh, why had she agreed to six-thirty?

Somewhat proud of herself, she pulled into her old home drive at exactly six forty-seven. Not too bad considering she'd stopped for coffee and donuts.

Samuel strolled out the front door sporting a heavy leather tool belt, hard hat, same jeans and shirt as yesterday—she could tell by the hole at his knee—but instead of his cowboy boots, he wore lace-up, thick-soled work footwear, probably steel toed, too.

He smiled, or rather smirked. "Hey, Boss, afternoon. Sleep well?"

She ignored him. "Watch yourself, I have hot coffee and donuts; you care for a bit of sugar?"

"Love some."

She held out the paper cup. "It's black." Sucking in her tummy to make digging in her jean pocket easier, she brought out a handful of packets then passed those to him, too.

"Great. Thanks."

She retrieved the box from her front seat, opened it, and held it toward him. He reached, but she jerked it back. "Take back your afternoon comment. You know it isn't true. The sun is barely up."

For a moment, his baby blues bore into her, then he grinned. "Okay. Good morning. How's that?"

"Better. Now what do you want me to do first?" She extended the box again and held it steady. He ate the three she got for him and one of hers, but Lord knew she didn't need it.

By ten-thirty, she'd changed her mind about the sugar she'd given away. Just watching the man would have worn her out, but he had her fetching tools and wood blocks she could barely lift.

Pulling and pushing, she worked like a dog. He even made her crawl under the house to slide him another jack because the one he had on that corner wasn't enough.

Then, like the Good Lord knew how bad she needed a break, the bee man came and once she discussed where he thought the best place for her new hive would be, Samuel sent her to town for materials and dinner.

Never had she ever been so tired and so hungry and so glad to sit down, even if it was in his old truck. She'd been eyeing that old blue chair all morning, but didn't figure it'd be nice to sit in it, leaving him to sit on the floor. Had to remember to scrounge up another one.

How could he stand his truck so dirty and messy? Mercy, the man needed someone. And how long had he been wearing the same clothes? But he smelled so good, how'd he pull that off?

Too soon, he wolfed down his burger and fries and swilled his sweet tea until the straw sucked air then went to crunching the ice. "Ready, Boss? Once we sister that main joist, I think we'll be in good shape to get serious about raising her up."

"How do you sister a joist?"

"With the two-by-twelves in the back of my truck." He nodded outside.

"Okay, what do we do with them?"

"I'll join them on both sides of the main floor joist, and that's what the old timers call sistering."

"Oh. And like that makes it stronger?"

"Yes, ma'am." He stood. "You ready?"

She really wasn't but stepped out onto the roll bar anyway. "Okay, so what's your plan and what's my part?"

He chuckled. "You look plum tuckered. Need a nap?"

"Nope, just tell me what for, and I'll do it or die."

"Now your demise is not necessary. Seriously, I can make do for the rest of the day."

"Oh, I'm okay." She walked around to the back of the truck and slid a board out over the tailgate. It weighed way more than she thought, and the far end hit the gravel. She looked up and grinned. "Ooops, heavier than I counted on."

"I'll get them in place, and then you can shove them to me after I'm back under the house."

She did as told, but that nap sounded so good. Wasn't about to quit on him though, after all it was her place, and she was the boss. She'd do whatever it took.

Exactly like he planned, the sistered two-by-twelves did the trick, and by quitting time, he had disconnected all pipes and successfully jacked up the whole house a good three inches.

"So is she high enough to move now?"

"Not yet, I'm going to need more blocks, but –" He snapped his fingers and clucked like he was getting up his cow pony.

"What?"

He unbuckled his belt and stowed it in his tool box then faced her. "I forgot to tell you, I spent some of your money. Guess the donut thing threw me off, but anyway Chucky's coming tomorrow afternoon."

She wanted to sit down in that old padded blue dining chair, but was afraid she'd never get up again. "Who's Chucky? And why's he coming? Will I need cash to pay him, or will he take my check?"

"Cash is always good. He's renting us his set of axles and I-beams. One of my hunting buddies, he's got the best string of hog dogs in Red River County. Met him out at the depot."

"You worked at the depot? Doing what?"

"Did some welding for them, but only for six months or so after PawPaw went home. He racked up some pretty good medical bills out at the hospital, and well… I hated it but it paid way better than day work." He opened the door to her sedan and nodded for her to get in.

"I'm sorry I wasn't here for his funeral, Samuel."

He threw her a forget it shrug. "Anyway, I hated welding all day long."

She took his hand and let him help her sit, but she didn't swing her feet in. How could anyone do something they hated for six months? But then she also understood him wanting to pay off the old man's final bills.

"How's your parents? You see them much?"

"No, Dad made the funeral, but didn't stay long. He was racing pretty fast."

"They still chasing the dragon?"

"Yep, working on their testimony. Some day, but doesn't look like it's this one." He closed his eyes. His lips moved as though praying, then he smiled. "How's your mother? I totally forgot to ask about her."

"Oh, she's good. Remarried. A nice man. They run a small hotel a few miles out of Denver; cater to the cross-country skiers. Have a drop-off, pick-up service."

"What does she think about all of this?" He waved at the old girl.

"Haven't told her."

"Really? Isn't the place hers or at least half or…." His face reddened a bit like he wanted to suck his words back.

"No, it's been in Daddy's family forever, and… oh, I guess it's been ten years now, but Gran left it to me, so no, it's all mine."

"Well, how about you. What say we call it a day? You look past tuckered. What time tomorrow?"

She swung her legs in then rolled down her window. "You tell me."

He leaned in but not too close. "With Chucky coming, figured I best get an early start."

"Six-thirty isn't early?"

"Not really, more like mid-morning most days."

She hated to ask, but did anyway. "Okay, so what time you planning on getting here?"

"Five or so."

"I'll be here. Want donuts?"

"Sure. And coffee, one cream and half a sugar."

"Got it." She patted his arm. "See you tomorrow then."

He backed away and she made herself drive off. All the way back to town she rehashed the day. Couldn't remember the last time she'd worked so hard—if she ever had.

But not once did he even seem winded or the least bit tired. For all she knew, he was planning on grabbing a quick nap then hunting hogs all night, except he had to be worn out, didn't he?

Lord knew, tired as she was, the strange bed wouldn't keep her awake an extra minute tonight. Matter of fact, maybe she'd just skip supper and crawl into it. She loved reading a little at bedtime, but no way that night.

Probably couldn't get through a page. No, sir, wouldn't need anything to help her doze off.

After a hot shower, a bit of cheese and crackers with a side of juicy apple slices, she sat in the wingback chair and actually kept her eyes opened through two chapters of Holly Michael's newest novel. That's all though she hated closing the book.

Then her hypothesis proved true. Exactly as predicted, she fell asleep almost before her head hit the pillow.

✝♥♫♪ •*•♪♫✝

All the way to English, Sam replayed the day, laughed again at her jerking the donut box back. For sure he wouldn't, but couldn't deny the temptation to slow down and make this house moving deal last.

But that wasn't his way.

PawPaw would roll over in his grave if he knew Samuel didn't put his alls on whatever the task at hand happened to be.

'Take a man's money, you give him your best.' The old man's words still rang in his mind's ear. Bless his heart, he'd taught him a good way to live.

Sam showered then decided to do some washing. First thing, she noticed him wearing yesterday's clothes, even though she tried to hide it. And he hated it that he'd forgotten how messy and dirty his truck was when he sent her to town.

But he did get a lot done while she was gone, and the trip seemed to perk her up some.

The hot water definitely helped his aches and pains, but instead of a second shower, he snuggled in bed and pulled his spiral notebook from the little cubbyhole in his headboard. He flipped to the last page he'd worked on and hovered his pen over the paper only a few seconds.

Praise God, Mary Esther, seems you've come home to stay, don't know why, but I'm sure glad you're here, if your mother would only show up with a monopoly game it'd be just like old times...

Before he finished that page, he drifted off.

As most nights, he dreamed, but this one starred two really old people sitting on a wrap-around porch in twin rocking chairs. For the longest, he watched the aged couple, before realizing he was the old man. He tried to stand up, but his legs wouldn't or couldn't work.

The lady looked at him and smiled. "You best wake up and get this house moved, or there will never be an 'us' in your future."

He bolted upright. He recognized her. The old lady was Mary Esther. He shook off the night vision. Was it a dream? Or only his silly self telling him his future rode on getting her house moved?

✝♥♫♪ *Chapter Three*

Mary Esther arrived that second morning with five whole minutes to spare. She spotted the light once she rounded the last curve then his truck. Of course he'd beat her. Did the man ever sleep?

She parked, followed the illumination to where he worked under the house, knelt, then peered in. "Hey, I got coffee and donuts. You hungry?"

"Morning, boss. I'll be out in a minute."

The one turned into three, but after he dusted himself off, he joined her in the carport. Took the coffee, one sugar packet and the two little cream buckets then went to work on the glazed, but left the chocolate for her.

Did he remember or just prefer the plain ones?

"We've got a problem, Boss."

She focused on him and stored his donut preferences. "What's that?"

"It dawned on me this morning, we have to haul the old girl longwise, but we may have to put her in place sideways."

"How hard is that?"

"Won't be easy. It's been a while since I was over there, but unless you've lost some trees…" He shrugged. "Thought we best go check it out."

She glanced eastward where false dawn coaxed the new day into the sky. "Sure, let's go see. This is exciting."

He strolled to the passenger side of his truck and opened the door. None of the trash and most of the dirt no longer littered the vehicle.

"Wow, looks like your cleaning lady came last night."

"Whatever." He hurried around to his side. Where he got the extra energy to move that fast, she did not know.

Once past the field her daddy called the twenty-two—he called most of his fields by the number of acres in them. Samuel turned right and followed the old County Road that bordered her property.

He stopped abruptly and pointed south. "Deer."

She followed his finger searching the trees that separated the twelve-acre field from the woods where she planned to move the house. Her mind's eye remembered it planted with corn.

She loved how straight Daddy's crop rows always ran. They seemed to go on forever and driving back toward the trees, she reminisced, peering down the whole length of each.

A whitetail flicked and brought her back to the present. She spotted the doe first then her twin yearlings. The three stood in the knee-high grass and weeds. For a while she watched.

"In the glove box, there's a pair of binoculars."

Moving in slow motion, she retrieved them, but by the time she twirled the lenses into focus, something spooked the trio. She lowered the field glasses and enjoyed them bounding away into the woods, her woods.

"Oh, I have sure missed seeing that."

"I never understood why you didn't come back. I mean even for a visit."

Her face warmed. Silence filled the cab of his truck like helium in a balloon, and it seemed the latex might burst at any moment. How could she explain? Her cheeks burned, they had to be rose red.

Mere seconds before any explosion, he spoke up, graciously changing the subject. "So what happened to that Yankee farmer? Thought at first ya'll had sold it, but heard tell he only leased the farmland."

"Apparently left town. FSA folks said the last time they saw him was when he picked up his base payment check."

"What are you going to do with it?"

"I don't know. No one seems to want it for farming. According to them, the soil report claims it needs to be limed and the fertility is way down. He probably didn't put any fertilizer on it." She glanced over at him. "Why? Know anyone looking for some acreage?"

"What about hay?"

"Well, I don't know, what about it? Think I could make some money?"

"Depends, but not as much as leasing it out as farm land—even if you had to pay half or all of the lime. Hay's first cutting wouldn't bring much more than cost, but after that, you might be looking at seven, maybe eight an acre, more if you're custom cutting and selling the rolls."

"Well, I need to do something; I've been paying the taxes on it with the CRP and farm lease dollars."

She hated the Crop Reduction Program—or thinking about money at all; seemed she'd been on the edge forever, but since the band's sales had grown, she'd been socking cash away every chance she got. Now that she did have some extra.

Thinking she could live on the old home place and spending the bulk of her reserve could prove to be an insane idea.

She opened the glove box then froze. Right there was all three of the band's CDs. She didn't look over at him, but put the glasses back then closed it. Did he really like her music or just buy them because he knew her?

Either way, she liked knowing he had them and thinking he listened to them all the time.

Of course, could be he played them once then forgot about them.

He neared the hidden entrance into the trees. The drive looked as though it ended at the tree line because of the second stand of trees making the first seem solid, but he passed into the hidden opening and immediately turned left. He weaved his way back on the trail that ran along the edge of the creek.

Rounding the last curve, the pool came into view. She smiled to herself. In Dallas concrete-formed walls and crystal clear blue water filled pools in the backyards of big homes, but not a one could hold a candle to her natural dirt one.

"Oh, bless the Lord! I love it back here."

"Yes, ma'am. It's a pretty building site alright." He grinned. "Remember your dad saying he'd dug that pool almost to China?"

She nodded and smiled. "Indeed he did. That's what I want to see out of my kitchen window."

He killed the engine, jumped out, then ran around and opened her door. He better watch out, she could sure get used to being treated like a lady. Couldn't remember the last time she had so much gentlemanly attention.

She walked halfway back then turned around. "You're right. I couldn't stand losing any of these oaks. The house needs to be right there."

"I agree." He turned around. "What a peace you'll have." He looked back to her. "We can put a big porch on the old girl once we get her here; wrap it all the way around if you want."

She loved the idea, but how much would that cost? "So you think we can get the house back here?"

"Oh sure. Might have to lose a few small trees." He pointed to a big leafless oak. "Looks like that one's dead, but it would have to come down anyway, so that's good. Might want to get Chucky involved."

"I forgot. You never said how much cash I need for him this afternoon."

"Three hundred."

"No problem. And what's that getting me?"

"Delivery, pick-up, and a week's rental."

"That's not too bad."

"There's more though."

"More? More what?"

"He insisted on a sweetener."

"Like what?"

"Hunting, says he wants to take you hogging."

"Me? Why in the world?"

"He thinks it'll make a great story. You're like the most famous person from here since… maybe since Dan Blocker."

"Who?"

"You know. Hoss! The heavy-set son on the Ponderosa."

"Are you talking Bonanza?" She laughed. "Sure! Ponderosa is what they called their ranch. Daddy loved that show."

"Whatever."

"So you're saying Hoss Cartwright was from Clarksville?"

"No, DeKalb, but close enough."

"Well, I am not a hunter, and I hate those ugly hogs. Everyone up here does, right? Would you be going with us?"

"Oh, absolutely. Chucky is okay, but...." He shrugged. "I wouldn't trust him with my sister if I had one."

Sister? He's thinking of her as a sister, understandable she guessed. They'd been so close as youngsters, best of friends. But what about that kiss he stole? That didn't seem at all like a sisterly kiss.

She'd slapped him hard, surprised her at the time how badly it stung her hand. She wouldn't slap him if he tried again. How much more would it cost her without the hunting trip?

"What's wrong? I wouldn't let anything happen to you."

"I hate money."

"What? Where'd that come from?"

She waved him off. "Okay, I'll go, but he has to help with the move."

"Last I heard he values his time at two fifty a day."

"I think we ought to get a discount, seeing as how I'm so famous and all." She laughed again and shook her head. That consideration was absurd. "Maybe throw in an extra hunt."

✞ ♥ ♫♪ •*•♪ ♫ ✞

Samuel loved that laugh, hadn't changed a bit since they were six years old, one of the reasons he fell in love with her. He held her door then hurried around to his side. Such an idiot. Why in the green earth would he compare her to a sister?

And that look in her eyes; exactly what was that?

And leaving those CDs in the glove box? Had to do better. Worse than an idiot, he was a gold-plated moron.

If she ran off again, he'd have no one but himself to blame. He'd lost her once. Why had he thought she wanted him to kiss her? If only he had a time machine, he could go back and fix it all. Keep her dad from going to Paris that day.

Then she would never have moved away, and he could have taken things nice and slow with her.

But no. Her dad got himself killed changing a lady's flat tire, and Mary Esther left the county. If he hadn't have stolen that kiss, maybe she would have answered his letters.

"Penny for your thoughts."

"What?" He looked over. How could one human being look so good?

Mercy, Lord, soften her heart toward me.

"Just now. What were you thinking about?" She chuckled. "You seemed to be a million miles away."

"Actually, your father." He shook his head. "I hated it that he got killed doing a good deed. Wasn't right."

"I know, nothing was right about it, not one thing. For the longest, I couldn't talk about him without crying, but life goes on. I miss him every day, but he's in a better place."

He nodded, though to him, being wherever she was made it like a bit of heaven coming right down to earth.

Oh Lord, please help me keep my foot out of my mouth.

"Now on the other hand, PawPaw was ready, and after he'd suffered so long, so was I. Just terrible, hated him hurting so bad. At the end, the morphine wasn't even cutting it."

"I just hate hearing that."

He could hardly stand thinking of it and sighed. "Him going home was a blessing."

"How old was he?"

"Eighty-three."

"That's a good long life. I'd take that, but I certainly don't want to have to suffer. I'd rather go in my sleep or a heart attack, something quick."

"Who wouldn't? Your dad didn't have to suffer."

She took a deep breath and let it out real slow. "So they said."

He nodded. He'd be fine with eighty-plus years, too, especially if she spent those last years rocking on the front porch he'd build on her house—with him. What about that? Would he hate moving from English?

Maybe they could split the time. Naw, she'd never want to live in his trailer, and PawPaw's old house wasn't worth rehabbing.

"Hey, where are you going?"

He came to himself, slammed on the brakes, then backed up. "Sorry, boss. Got lost in thought. Thinking about PawPaw does me that way. Guess I have the automatic pilot on, headed for home."

In no time, he got back at it. If he could jack the old girl high enough, maybe he could get Chucky to wench it all in place, just dropping everything would sure make it hard on him.

He probably would want more money, but Mary Esther agreeing to go hogging might grease his wheels a bit. After the second trip around the house, cranking each hydraulic jack five times, she stopped him at the carport.

"Ready for lunnn... dinner?"

"I could eat."

"What do you want?"

"Doesn't matter, surprise me."

"Need anything from the lumber yard?"

"No, we're good for now."

While she was gone, he got the house up another block's worth, but then had to reposition each jack, and that took too long.

Lord, strengthen me, this up and down and...

He rubbed his right shoulder and neck. Mercy, why couldn't she have bought herself a nice herd of Angus she needed help with? This house moving was about to do him in. The remodeling would be better, get out from under and inside instead.

Cold cuts, but not slap a slice of baloney on two pieces of bread and calling it a sandwich. She brought smoked turkey and honey ham on ten grain bread with pickles, onions, tomatoes, and lettuce, plus three cheeses to choose from.

Probably been cheaper to buy a steak. That's what he needed to do, bring his grill over and smoke her some barbeque.

"Tomorrow, I'll fix dinner."

She cocked her head and shot him a quizzical look. "You don't like my sandwiches?"

"No, they're great. Best I've had in… maybe ever, but I been thinking. You probably spent so much on this spread, a steak would have been as cheap. But then we wouldn't have any way to cook it, so…."

"I see how you are."

He smiled. "I'll bring my smoker; wait until you taste my ribs."

"Sounds great. What are we going to have with them? You bring your smoker and ribs, I'll get everything else."

"Potatoes, we can smoke them on the grill, and fresh corn on the cob or anything you want, I can heat it up."

While he ate a third gourmet sandwich, she over-planned tomorrow's dinner, but it should be fun, and he could leave his rig there. Wasn't like he'd be using it anywhere else—at least for a while.

Too soon, he had to stop stealing glances and get back to work. He'd hired out by the day, not the hour, and dinner meant however long it took to grab some grub, not lollygagging around an hour. He hated watching a clock.

Worst part of working at the depot was punching in and out, having to leave projects unfinished. Praise God, he'd put that job behind him. He could make enough to live on working for the other man until he could build his herd to the point where he could live off his calf crop.

He stopped a bit before four. Hopefully, he had her high enough to get the axles and rails under the old girl. Chucky should be there any minute.

Like he figured, his bud arrived a bit past four, but then after him taking one look at Mary Esther and her smiling back at him, Samuel wished he'd never invited Chucky to be anywhere near her.

Chapter Four ✝♥♫♪

After introductions and Samuel's friend gushing too much over her, Mary Esther decided time to 'get after it' had arrived; she nodded toward his truck and the rig he towed behind. "How does this all work?"

"We drop the rails and one set of axles on this end of the house, take the other set around to the north side then winch it all together."

He gave her a you're-stupid smile, one that said only because he liked her he answered her totally idiotic question. She hated it when guys did that, even if they were handsome.

She sang for the money that bankrolled the move of her house, and would pay plenty for his equipment and services—not to mention hunting his stupid hogs. Still, she offered him her best stage smile and nodded as though she understood exactly what was about to happen.

As it played out it made sense, amazing indeed, that in less than an hour, the fellows had the house ready to roll, but then she and Samuel had accomplished all the hard prep work before Chucky ever showed.

He squirted a blob of hand cleaner in Samuel's waiting palm then one in his own.

The newcomer smiled at Mary Esther, not exactly an expression of being pleased or happy, neither a come-on. What did the odd gesture mean to convey? Then she burst out laughing. The men looked at her, then each other

Samuel wiped his hands on a rag towel. "What's funny?"

She regained her composure. "Yes, nothing, it's me. For a second… It's just I couldn't figure… It was only a please-feed-me look, but sorry." She glanced at Chucky. "It didn't register at first. Three hundred cash, is that right?"

"Yes, ma'am, thanks. When should I bring the dogs?"

She retrieved her purse, counted out the money, then held it out. "Oh, I don't know." She faced Samuel. "When do you want to go?"

His buddy took the dollars. "When did he get invited?"

She laughed again. "He's my protector. Hear tell you're not a man a lady should be left alone with." She shrugged. "Guess any night is as good as another."

He looked from her to Samuel, then expelled a heavy sigh. "Fine, I suppose. How does night after next sound?"

She checked her mental calendar. "Okay, today's Wednesday, so we're talking Friday evening. What time?"

"Yes, ma'am, how about six?"

She extended her hand. "Six it is. You coming to help us this weekend? Samuel thinks we might need an extra hand to get my house in place."

There he went with his unreadable expressions again. Finally, he grinned at Samuel who nodded. The man shrugged. "Sure, why not? I get three hundred a day."

She let her hand fall to her side. "Really? I heard it was less. How about half that and found. I make a mean sandwich." She winked at Samuel.

"Okay, sure. I'll take a buck fifty if you'll sing at church on Sunday. What do you say?"

"I could do that. Where do you go?"

"Well." He backed up a step. "Actually, my mother asked me to ask you. She goes to the DeKalb Church of Christ."

"I'd love to. We'll see you Friday at six."

Seemed to her, Samuel couldn't get his friend loaded up and gone too soon. What happened to shooting the breeze? Thought visiting was the main stay of country folks. Sure had always been her mother's favorite pastime.

Once the old truck drove off, Samuel sidled up to her. "Sure like the way you put him in his place. Did you see how flustered he got?"

"Not really. I did notice all the glares you kept shooting his way. If looks could kill, the poor man would be dead." She poked his arm. "Trying to protect your sister?"

He laughed. "You have not changed one iota."

What exactly did that mean? Why didn't he tell her not at all, that he'd never thought of her as a sister. Apparently that's how he saw her, as a platonic relationship between such good childhood friends…except…why had he kissed her that day? What? Twenty years ago?

Mercy, she was going crazy. Still… Was that what this was all about?

She should have said something. The silence grew a bit suffocating.

He finally said something. "I've got to go."

She nodded. "Okay, it's been a long day. I'm tired, too."

"It has been a long day, but I've got to get to Big Woods. I'm subbing tonight for Jake."

"Mercy, Samuel, you can't work day and night."

"No, Jake teaches the Wednesday night Bible class at the Big Woods Community Church; asked me to catch out for him tonight. He had a hot shot to Oklahoma City and didn't see how he could get back in time."

"Cool, can I go?"

"I'd like that. But we best get a move on then. Starts at seven-thirty."

"So how do I get there?"

"If you don't know, trust me, you'd never make it. Remember where Avery is?"

"Between here and DeKalb on 82?"

"Yes, meet me there at the blinking light. You can leave your car at the store. Think you can make it by seven?"

She punched her phone to life. She really needed a shower. "Maybe; I can try. What's your number if I'm running late."

"Don't have one."

"What? You don't have a phone?"

"I've got a house line, but no cell."

"Why not?"

He shrugged. "Long story. I'll wait until seven ten, but then I'll have to go."

"Okay, I'll hurry."

On the way back to town, she ticked off what she'd could and couldn't do to make it by seven. Forget washing her hair, or taking any time to assemble an ensemble, not like she'd be performing.

Oh wow. A pang of conviction stabbed her heart. Oh, God. Repentance washed over her and she gave it voice. Was that what she'd been doing on the road? Only performing?

Once, no more than singing God's praises and loving on Him mattered.

When had it turned into a show?

Thank You, Lord, for revealing this and for Your forgiveness.

Avery's blinking light came into view at six past seven. He stood beside his truck. Four minutes to spare. He motioned for her to park in front of the little store. She pulled in, hurried to his opened passenger door, then slid in.

He checked the traffic then eased out before saying anything. "Sure proud you made it."

"Me, too. You do this much, teaching Bible classes?"

"Some, even get to preach now and again, but nothing regular."

"Wow, that's great, Samuel."

She leaned back in the seat. Why Lord did you take me away from this man? What if Daddy had lived? Would she and Samuel still be together?

"What's wrong?"

She turned sideways in her seat. "Oh, just playing what-if I guess, asking God for maybe the millionth time why Daddy had to die."

"I try not to do that. Can't change the past. Don't always get what I want either."

"Tell me about it." She sliced the air. "Different subject, actually two. Why no cell phone? It is the twenty-first century, you know. And second, what are you teaching on tonight?"

He snickered.

"What's so funny? Are you laughing at me?"

"No, usually the questions come three at a time. Just now it was only two."

She resisted poking his arm. "What? You've got a problem with asking questions?"

"No. I had a cell. Once. Took a hammer to it after the first bill arrived. Had to sell a calf before I was ready to pay the thing off and buy out the stupid contract I signed."

"Yikes."

"So guess it wasn't that long of a story. Anyway, most everyone knows where I live, and I do have the same old house line."

She pulled out her phone. "What's that number?"

He told her, and she saved it. "Okay, what are you teaching on?"

"Not sure. Jake said whatever I wanted, so I'm doing what the Lord said."

She searched, but no scripture bells went off. "And what's that? What are you talking about?"

"You know. Taking no thought. For what you're going to say. The Holy Ghost will give you the words you need."

"Wasn't he referring to when they take you before the king?"

"Actually, more like synagogues, magistrates, and powers, but good guys or bad, works the same."

"So you don't have anything prepared?"

"Nope, sometimes the Lord will give me something ahead of time. But tonight, no. I don't have a clue. It's always fun seeing what the Lord has planned."

"Mercy, I couldn't do that. We'd practice and practice then practice some more." She shook her head. "I wanted each and every show planned out, every song, no surprises."

Her own words knifed her heart. She'd never thought of it before like that. Could it be that she wanted her own way? Control, instead of allowing any room for the Holy Spirit to do what He wanted?

The blacktop ran out, but he didn't slow a bit. Two curves later, he pulled into a surprisingly big, one-story church complex. What looked to be a sanctuary with a taller roof by six foot or so and two wings, one on each side.

Maybe class rooms to the west, fellowship hall the other. Different, but also like so many others. She loved church, loved getting together with fellow believers. Hopefully, the ladies didn't bring many killer deserts.

That was one thing she hated—and loved—about being on the road. And she needed such temptations like she needed a married associate pastor in her hotel room.

What a jerk.

Samuel eased around to the back. Better than a dozen cars and trucks already dotted the lot. Some in close, others out on the grass.

Why did country folks play like their lawns were parking spaces and pastures were green roads? In town, the police would at least issue a citation, and at worst, tow the car for parking on the owner's own grass.

At first, everyone seemed only to focus only on Samuel, gushing about how happy they were that he'd agreed to fill in.

Then a lady maybe her mother's age—so hard for her to judge—did a double take and pointed at her as if pointing was polite and absolutely socially acceptable—especially when all of the sudden, you'd spotted a celebrity.

"You're Mary Esther Robbins."

She smiled. "Yes, ma'am."

"You're the Mary Esther, right? The singer?"

"Yes, ma'am. One and the same. Guilty."

"Well, how about us! What are you doing here? Shouldn't you be… on tour or something?" The lady did a circle motion mostly westward, like she expected Mary Esther to fill in the blanks.

"I live here now."

"Really? I'd heard that you were from around here, but that you left after… Um, so where, exactly?"

"Clarksville. I have a place a few miles south out of town on Peter's Prairie Road."

"Well now, isn't that something? You've come home. And how is it you know our Samuel?"

He cleared his throat, and she glanced over and smiled. "Well, they kicked me out of kindergarten, and there he sat in the back row all cute as a first grader could possibly be. We were best friends through elementary. I left our first year in middle school."

"Evening, Mrs. Hooker." He slid in next to her and extended his hand.

The lady took it in both of hers. "I'm so proud you brought Mary Esther tonight. You two make an adorable couple."

He grinned like he was six years old again, and his cheeks reddened. "Uh, thanks. Guess we best get started."

"Of course." Mrs. Hooker nodded toward two front row chairs. "I always like to be where the action is. Come on, sit with me, Mary Esther."

Samuel got everyone settled down then after opening with a short prayer, stopped and closed his eyes for too long. Mrs. Hooker started praying under her breath. Mary Esther heard others, too, and bowed her head to join, asking for God's Kingdom to come on earth at the Big Woods Community Church, for His will to be done there.

Finally, her childhood friend broke the silence. "The godless fear death, lust for power, and hate anyone who threatens either." He looked at the almost two dozen folks.

She loved the sound of his voice, but the way he taught— definitely anointed, beyond anything she expected. He quoted scripture, engaged his audience, drew out amens, and made point after excellent point.

Mercy, she'd sat under some of the best-known preachers and teachers across the country, but not a one of them had anything on Samuel Baylor.

He finished with a phrase that sent her creative juices flowing. Like so often, it all came at once as though God wrote it on her heart from one to beat to the next.

"Mary Esther?"

Him speaking her name brought her back, and she focused on him. Had he asked her a question? "I'm sorry, what?"

"Would you grace us with a song?"

The no died on her lips. She hadn't prepared anything, but should that make a difference? Neither had he, and it had been great. "Will you help me?"

"Help you sing?" He chuckled. "I'm liable to throw you off. I have trouble staying on key."

She held her hand out. "No, I've got something else in mind."

"Okay." He pulled her to her feet, tried to let go, but she held on.

She kept her back to the crowd, pushed him a bit then eased his near ear down. "Start with what you just said about them thinking they had Jesus. Whenever I squeeze your hand, you stop. Then whenever you squeeze mine, I'll stop."

"What song?"

"You'll see. If I'm right, it'll be great." She turned and squeezed his hand. Standing next to the man about to jump off into what the Spirit led…

"They thought they had this unschooled, upstart prophet from Nazareth. Who did the young rabbi think he was? Not even a scribe, much less a priest. They'd show him. And best of all, the Romans would do their dirty work for them."

Unable to keep from smiling, she covered her mouth and cleared her throat. He really got into it.

"Forget stoning Him, that'd be too easy. Let Him hang naked on a cross for a while. See how the self-proclaimed king took that."

She squeezed his hand and sang, "Up from the grave He arose, with a mighty triumph o'er His foes."

He echoed, "He arose." But didn't squeeze her hand.

She smiled at him and continued right where she left off. "He arose the Victor from the dark domain. And lives forever with His saints to reign. He arose!"

"He arose."

"He arose!"

"He arose."

Until then, she'd sung the old hymn just as she had as a child, but suddenly, she heard the angels singing and could do nothing more than join in with them—what she heard. "Halle-looooo-ia. Ha-ah ah ah ah-le-lu-ia. He arose from the grave, triumphant all to save. He died for me, died just for me. He died for you, died just for you." She squeezed his hand.

Back and forth, he talked, and she sang the hymn as written. The favorite Resurrection Sunday tradition with a whole new arrangement. The folks ate it up, hung on every word, every note, basking in the presence of God.

Then he motioned them to join in. Too soon, he slipped his hand from hers. She let the last note fade.

How had she remembered all those verses? Or had she made them up?

For a second, no one spoke. A few hands wiped tears. An old man in the back started clapping. When had he come in? Spontaneous praise erupted, and the shouting and clapping went on for what seemed like forever.

But still, she was sorry for it to end.

Everyone either shook his hand or told her how much they enjoyed her singing. Somehow, he extracted her from the well wishers with several it's-getting-lates, a few have-to-get-up-so-earlys, and one rather nasty the-lady's-working-me-like-a-dog.

Once the truck reached blacktop and its tires' song mellowed out, he glanced at her. "That was awesome."

She nodded. "It was, wasn't it?" 'My love' almost slipped out, but echoed only in her heart, not her ears. She couldn't give it voice. She had no right after slapping him that day. He promised to write, but never had.

The disappointment at the mailbox day after day, through all the seasons....

Why, Lord? Why?

✝♥♫♪ Chapter Five

Samuel watched her taillights until they got smaller moving west on 82. Parting wasn't sweet sorrow, only heartache. Soar to the mountain top with the Lord then come crashing back down with her leaving.

Again. Except this was worse; her own free will and volition. The prime opportunity presented itself, but did he say anything? No. He was such a coward. Why couldn't he share his heart?

All the way back to English, he beat himself up over not telling her how thrilled her coming home made him, how much he enjoyed her company, working with her, her sassy and fun discussions.

He wanted to let her know he still loved her and always would, that she was his first love and if he had anything to say about it, would be his last.

But no, he couldn't even bring himself to let her know how hurtful it had been when the three letters he'd sent her came back marked address unknown. He'd double, no triple-checked that he'd written the exact address she gave him.

She never read them. He'd tried to convince himself maybe her mother sent them back. But why would she?

He rubbed his cheek. Why had he kissed her that day? At least he knew the answer to that question, or part of it anyway. Because he'd been afraid he wouldn't see her again for a long time, and she needed to know how much he loved her.

Never should have. He'd always regretted it and apologized in every letter, asked for her forgiveness.

Her taillights went around a bend and out of sight. Letting out a heavy sigh, he hopped into his truck and whistled Up From the Grave He Arose!

That night after he finally found sleep, he dreamed again of the old couple. Though he never could see either face clearly, he instinctively sensed he was the old man.

Then an old Chucky stepped up onto the porch and squeezed in between him and Mary Esther. "Sorry, buddy, but I got dibs."

Samuel sat up, relieved. Only a dream. The bedside clock read three-thirty-three. Three threes. What did that mean? He flopped back down, but the day's projects kept calling to be planned, and it sure wouldn't hurt to pray extra. Lord knew he needed all the help and encouraging words he could get.

✞ ♥ ♫♪ •*•♪ ♫ ✞

If Mary Ester dreamed that night, she didn't remember. The church meeting the night before played over in her mind that next morning as she puttered around her temporary room trying to decide exactly what to wear.

Had the service held some clandestine meaning? She needed to do some laundry or find a drop-off service.

She had no clue what that might cost. Or if Clarksville even had one. Sure wasn't the bustling small town she'd known as a child. Bless God, her handsome contractor had agreed to a more reasonable start time, especially since church had run long. She smiled.

To hear him tell it, seven-thirty was mid-afternoon.

All the way back to Avery, she'd given him so many opportunities to spill his guts, but all he wanted to talk about was how awesome the duet on that number sounded and how much he enjoyed it.

Well, of course it was, but that's not what she wanted to talk about. She wanted to discuss her and him, if any chance for a relationship even existed anymore.

She loved it when Mrs. Hooker said they made a cute couple, but then he hadn't made any comment. And worse, he hugged everyone there last night but her. No hello hug, no goodbye squeeze.

Mercy, he hadn't even shook her hand. He did open her car door, but seemed to avoid any physical contact.

She didn't want to pull one of his tricks and wear dirty jeans, besides, they got plenty grimy from working so hard. She chose her least favorite skirt and the same old blouse she usually wore with it.

If it got ruined, no big deal. Instead of donuts, she ran by Mickey D's and ordered three biscuits, six strawberry jelly packets, and two coffees.

His truck stood in her gravel drive. She pulled in and parked behind him. What would she have to do to ever beat him there? She called him out from under the house and handed over two of the biscuits.

"Good morning." Again, my love played on the tip of her tongue, but went unspoken. It tickled her that she kept thinking it though.

"Yes, it is." He unwrapped the first one and went to loading it with jelly. He grinned at her. "Thank you."

"You're welcome, but food was a part of the negotiations."

"Wasn't talking about the biscuits, but thanks for them, too."

"Then what are you talking about?"

"Your skirt. Not wearing jeans."

"Oh, please. Don't tell me you don't approve of jeans. Lord, Samuel, everyone wears them these days." She shook her head and took a bite, sucked out a little jelly from the torn corner of her packet, and chewed, but swallowed too soon.

Had he become a male chauvinist pig? Surely not.

She washed it down with the hot brew. "So what's wrong with a woman wearing jeans?"

He held his hands up. "Forgive me for saying anything." He globbed another squeeze of strawberry on and took on the second of his three-bite biscuit. Mercy, he inhaled the things.

"No, you started this, now tell me." She pinched off a small piece of hers, popped it in, and followed it with another petite suck off her packet.

"If you must know, I prefer skirts. That and the Word says for women not to wear men's clothes, well actually, anything that even pertains to a man."

She washed down another of her petite bites with coffee. "Oh, please, give it up. I'd like you to show me any man who could wear my Wranglers."

"Trust me, there are guys out there who'd love to have your jeans, but it's more than that. Who exactly are you dressing for? The Lord? Or to show off, get men to lust after you?"

"Samuel...."

His tone carried no condemnation. Quite calm and matter-of-factly, he sounded sweet and sincere even if she didn't like what he was saying.

Well, she did not buy her jeans in the men's section, but she did have to admit she'd stood in front of her mirror plenty of times admiring her girly curves in denim. She always had, at least since she could remember having curves.

Hmm, so maybe that wasn't so good.

"Could be you're only trying to intimidate other women wanting to show them how gorgeous you are."

He thinks I'm gorgeous. "So what? You want me in a burka?"

He grinned. "Got one?"

"No, don't be an idiot."

"Modesty is what the Word says." He pouted his bottom lip with a quick little shrug. "Dress like either one of your namesakes."

Several retorts came to mind, but she couldn't bring herself to argue. His words carried so much truth. She'd never really thought about it. Slipping into a pair of jeans came second nature. She wore them everywhere.

Also had a closet full of slacks, too. Guess he'd think the same of those.

Wow.

Could he be speaking for the father she'd been robbed of? She took herself another absent-minded bite. Would Daddy have said the same thing? Did all daddies tell their daughters such?

Tears welled, but she blinked them away. Samuel was not her father, but if not her earthly one, sounded like he might be talking for her heavenly Father for sure.

"You really think I shouldn't wear pants of any kind?"

He shrugged again, this time a bigger one. "Ask the Lord. He's the one who counts most. I can tell you it sure would make my life easier."

"Okay." She blew out a big breath, long and slow. "I'll pray about it. Now what do we need to do today?"

He popped the last bite of biscuit he'd been holding, then nodded sideways toward the house. "Looks to me she's ready to go. Best move our operation south."

"Cool, I'd wondered when we would start getting the new site ready. I am so excited." What do we need to do there?"

"Lay it all out, dig some pier holes, rough-in the plumbing; lots to do before we can move your house."

"I like a man with a plan." She glanced at his truck and the trailer hooked on behind it. "Has that been there all along?"

He chuckled. "You just now noticing? Brought my smoker and picnic table."

"Is that what that is? Sure, I noticed something, but I haven't been to the store."

He opened the driver's door to her sedan and stood aside. "Come on, line me out, then you can go shopping."

He had that right, she needed to do some serious shopping, and not just for sides. She owned a few church dresses, but not any other skirts or dresses she wanted to work in.

She grabbed his offered hand and stepped around. "What about the hunt? Am I supposed to go hogging in a dress, too?"

"Why not? Didn't figure you to be doing much anyway besides watching."

She eased in behind the wheel. "How about working calves? I've never sat a horse with anything on but jeans."

He held his hands out and shrugged. She loved that little shoulder motion he made, exactly like he'd done it when he was twelve. "Split skirts? Or a real full one? I don't know. I've never been a girl."

She grinned and nodded toward his truck, but couldn't keep her eyes from meeting his. "You going to follow me or stand there staring?"

He backed up as though his eyes acted as obstinate as hers. Bless his heart, he stumbled a bit, caught himself, then whirled around and jumped into his truck.

Half a mile or so south, she stopped short of where she wanted the house and jumped out. He joined her then pointed to a spot ten feet or so to her left. "How about the northeast corner right there?"

"Maybe, got any stakes?"

He threw her a smirk, then walked to the back of his truck and pulled out four long ones and a hammer. After only four false starts and lots of stepping off and measuring, he finally drove the fourth skinny pointed wooden marker at the last corner of the house's new home.

Then she held one end of his hundred-foot tape, while he squared it all up, hoping he'd explain how come he measured an X across the corners, but he didn't offer to, and it didn't really matter anyway.

He declared it right, and she had to agree it looked good to her. Inside the square, she hurried to the wall where her kitchen window would be, to check the view. Wow, it was going to be great, especially once all her remodeling was finished.

Oh, Lord, let the money last or bring in more.

She needed to call Brad's accountant, check on his progress figuring her royalties and road cut. The man didn't even have her new address. Drats, she hoped he hadn't mailed a check to the condo.

She focused on the now. "Okay, so sides...potatoes or corn? Want salad?"

"Whatever you like, I'm good, unless you want to take my truck and pick up some concrete blocks."

"If I get to choose, how about asparagus? Do you hate it?"

"Never ate it."

She smirked. "What are those blocks for? Thought we were pouring concrete."

"We are pouring piers, but the blocks go on top those." He waved her off. "Oh, never mind. There's a guy I know who has all kinds of used building materials. There's already plenty to do today. Go on to the store, and I'll get the ribs on."

What a deal. A man who could do it all, including cooking. Was there anything he couldn't do? She only thought a minute and harrumphed. For one, he apparently couldn't write a letter.

But then, she had slapped his face—hurt and insulted him when he was obviously only trying to show his affection. Was he still holding a grudge?

Cruising along Main Street toward Rehkoph's, the Vintaj Cowgirl shop on the square caught her eye. She drove around an extra block, made three rights then a left on Main Street and parked right in front of the store.

The old-timey display windows on both sides of the recessed door were full, and she loved them. Looked like the proprietor had great taste. Maybe she'd have some ideas on sitting a saddle in a skirt.

Mary Esther loved small towns.

After too much time and money—he'd been right, she shouldn't be going around in jeans—she made her way to the grocery store. After grabbing olive oil and fresh asparagus, tomatoes, green onions and cottage cheese, she decided to run by her room and put up her new things.

She smiled at herself.

He not only said she was gorgeous, he said the others couldn't compare.

♀♥♫♪ •*•♪♫♀

The dirt flew. Samuel hated digging, exactly like his PawPaw claimed. Shovels didn't fit his hand. He made himself go faster, just like his grandfather had taught him. If he had a distasteful job, do it as quickly as possible and be done with it. Do it right without lollygagging around, wishing it would go away.

He loved the old man's words echoing in his heart.

Still missed him, but some fine day, he'd be reunited with his most favorite person—no, better change that to man.

Mary Esther's coming back into his life reinforced what he'd known since first grade; she was his completion, his soul mate, the perfect one whom the Lord made for especially for him.

But did she know it? Had God revealed to her that Samuel was her match?

He needed to say something, but what if...?

Another shovelful, then another; while he worked, he contemplated the one area of his life his PawPaw had never advised him on. The old man claimed to know nothing about women. How could he?

Married to the same woman for forty-two years then never even having dinner with another one the rest of his life, he had no experience.

The Word said not to lust after the flesh, but was it still lust if you were totally in love with the object of your affection? How could he not want her? She was so....

"Stop it, man, think about what you're doing." He checked his work, all four corners dug out, the plumbing trench running west to the edge of the string line on a nice slope. Best check on the ribs, wouldn't do to burn them, especially after shooting his mouth off about how good they'd be.

After flipping them, he put on another stick of pecan wood in the firebox then eased the lid back down. What next? More digging. She sure had been gone a spell. How long did it take to get some veggies?

Each pier needed a three-foot hole, and of all the shovel work, holes were the worst. He retrieved his posthole digger and got busy. Another fifteen or twenty mother cows, and he could forget day labor.

"Fool, if you'd take the money the church folks offered you, wouldn't need to lift a finger." Clear as anything, the words weren't heard with his ears, but sounded loud in his spirit.

He slammed the digger into the new hole then waved both hands in front of his face. "Satan, get behind me. You know I've vowed never to merchandise the Gospel."

"No need to wear yourself out. It's okay." He recognized the same voice. "You know the workman is worth his hire."

Samuel pulled out another bite. "Hush up, that's probably the same thing you told Paul."

Now there's someone he'd like to have known. Next to the Lord himself, the apostle who penned most of the New Testament would be a strong number two.

Used to, he could so identify with the single, celibate man, but now, instead of a life alone, the Lord had brought Mary Esther back.

Oh, Father, work it all out. Your Word promises You'll give us the desires of our hearts. How long ago did you put the love for her in my heart?

He laughed out loud. And how many times had the Holy Spirit fanned those desires to give him strength when he needed it most?

So many folks got that scripture all wrong. If they wanted something bad, they thought it meant God would give it to them. Over the years, he'd disappointed a lot of confused Christians by explaining to them what that scripture really meant—at least as he understood it.

A flash of sunlight pulled him sideways. Her sedan rounded the corner. He grabbed another bite of dirt, pulled it out, then slammed the digger back in the hole and walked toward her. Best see what she bought, had to be mid-morning.

Her door opened, and she got out. He froze halfway to her. The new outfit she now wore looked awesome on her. Whether the color or the way it fit—modest, yes, but…

Oh, Lord. Maybe she needs that burka after all.

Or had her absence and return been what sent his heart racing?

Chapter Six ✞♥♫♪

Mary Esther kept a straight face, though the effort proved difficult. Behind it, she grinned ear to ear at his reaction to her new clothes. She loved the way he ogled her, that alone made letting him win the dress code debate.

The man gave her the impression she looked feminine enough in her new work skirt and blouse to pay off the national debt. Finally, his mouth closed and his feet moved toward her.

Beyond him more stakes, a string strung all the way around, and one across the middle over a trench—not to mention the four corners obviously dug pretty deep if the piles of dirt around each were any indication—evidenced his hard work while she'd been gone.

Hadn't seemed that long.

"Hey, is that a plumbing trench? Sure looks like you've been busy." The sweet aroma of roasting meat flooded her mouth with more saliva than a lady should have. That Mickey D's biscuit had made like a drop of water on the Texas prairie and vanished.

"It is, I have, and wow, I love your new outfit." He shook his head and looked toward her car. "What'd you get us?"

"Asparagus, makings of my delish cottage cheese salad, and a gallon of sweet Red Diamond tea."

"Sounds good, guess you figured the time had come for me to try the green spears."

She winked and hopefully sent the urge to hug her until she couldn't breathe all over him. "Sir, yes, sir!"

"How long does your salad take? The ribs are getting close."

"Oh, it practically makes itself. Chop the green onions, dice the tomatoes, stir, and salt and pepper."

"What do I need to do with the asparagus?"

"I'll dribble it with olive oil and season it, won't take long at all on the grill. Got us some plates, cups, and plastic ware for our picnic, too. That aroma you've got going...yum!"

He opened her back door and retrieved her grocery sacks. "Thanks, I should've got two racks so we'd have leftovers."

Not quick enough for her mouth, he had it all ready. Her sweetheart offered a short grace over the dinner, and she dug in. Not fair, no one should be able to smoke ribs that tasted like that.

Praise the Lord he'd only brought one rack or she'd have to keep eating until she exploded. And what was that extra flavor? She licked the last bit of sauce off her fingers. "Okay, my friend, I have to ask you to promise me something."

"What's that?"

"No more than twice a month. My figure couldn't stand this regular. I mean, I've never tasted anything like it. And that zinger flavor—secret sauce or what?"

"No, pecan."

"Like the nuts?"

"Naw." He grinned. "You're so cute. Well-seasoned wood. I've tried them all. Mesquite, hickory, red oak, bois d'arc. Nothing compares to pecan."

"Well I'm sold, best ribs ever. But I'm serious. I'd have to go buy a whole new wardrobe. They're that good. Ever thought about a restaurant?"

"Thank you, and no. I'll take note though. I like you exactly like you are."

"Really? Just like I am?"

He propped his elbows on the table, still holding a rib at both ends. "Yes, ma'am."

"Wouldn't change anything?"

"Not as long as you keep on dressing like you are right now." He held up his hands. "Hold it! There's one thing I'd change if you let me."

Okay, here it came. He'd grown into some kind of control freak—ban a pair of jeans here, who knows what he plans for there. "So what is it?"

"Your hair."

"My hair? What's wrong with my hair?" More irritation than she intended tinted her tone.

"Don't get me wrong. I love it. Just whoever trims it in the back, I'd like it better just natural than cut straight across. But truly, it's so minor. Doesn't matter. Your hair is fabulous."

"My mother trims my hair every time I see her; guess it's a thing she has, kind of like someone seeing a drip of mustard on your chin. I'd have to stop going around her."

"Like I said, no big deal. You're a ten either way."

She loved hearing him say it, but… "No, maybe a seven, but I'm no ten."

Half smile, half grimace etched his face, but not a speck of humor shone in his eyes. "Look, beauty is in the eye of the beholder, and if I say you're a ten, then you do not get to correct me." He chuckled.

"Whatever."

"To the men of that African tribe whose women put rings on their daughters' necks to make them freaky long, their wives are beautiful. They'd probably rate your short neck self a weak four, but they don't get a vote in my election."

Resisting the urge to pull him to his feet and smother him with kisses took great, huge, powerful strong self-control. That would have to wait, but what was he waiting for? Her to apologize?

He shouldn't have kissed her, not that day. Any other day might have been different, could be she would even have kissed him back.

But not that day.

Not with everyone there.

Not with her daddy going into the ground.

What if someone had seen them?

He stood. "Time waits for no man."

She focused. "What?"

He extended his hand. "Work, we need to get back at it."

"Yes, sir." She took his hand and let him pull her to her feet, but didn't let go. "Thank you. What did you think of the asparagus?"

"You're welcome; I love ribs, too. The spears were tasty enough. I can take them or leave them."

She laughed. "Thanks for cooking, too. But I was talking about you sticking to your ten. You're too sweet though, and you're going to give me a big head."

He laughed with her. "Oh, you're welcome." He tugged on her hand. "Come on, I'll introduce you to my spare posthole digger."

Maybe she managed to do one to his ten, she couldn't keep track. But then she was a girlie girl, and Samuel Baylor was the manliest man she'd ever run across. He'd grown up real well.

She leaned against the red oak that would be guarding her back porch. "How come?"

He pulled the diggers out, dropped what would come loose of the damp black dirt, then tapped the ends on the piece of two-by-four he'd retrieved for that purpose. "How come what?"

"You're not married. Mercy, Samuel, I've never known anyone who works like you do. I can't imagine why some country gal hasn't snapped you up."

"Thank you, or better yet, thank my PawPaw if you see him before I do. Just paying for my raising I guess. Train up a child and all that. And well…" He went back to his hole.

"Stop. I want to know. Really. That dirt you're working on isn't going anywhere. Give me the low down."

He slammed the diggers into the ground a ways from the hole then faced her. "You sure are bossy, but then you were always like that—a take-charge kind of girl. Remember when our second grade teacher, what was her name?

Anyway, she told Betsy Aikman she wasn't getting to go to the library and you marched straight to the principal's office and went to tattling on…"

"Miss Brice."

"Yeah, that was her name. And you started bossing him around telling him what he needed to do about her."

"She wasn't being fair! Mary Jo had read the extra books and earned the right to go to the library, and Miss Brice was wrong. So, I fixed it."

"Yes, you did." He turned toward his work.

"Wait."

He turned back. "What now?"

"Ha! I'm not that easy. You didn't answer my question. Are you avoiding it on purpose?"

"What a rude accusation."

"Yeah, well, how come you're not married?"

He shook his head. "Hey, it was worth a try. I didn't figure you'd let me change the subject though. The short of it would be my high standards. Seems these days, most ladies our age can't meet them."

"Like what? I mean what are your standards?"

He smiled. "Sold out, blood bought, virgin daughter of God-fearing parents."

"Wow, you do have high standards. Is that you or your grandfather talking?"

"Both, but time's a wasting. If we're going to move your house day after tomorrow, I need to get these holes dug."

"Why? If we have two days, what's the rush?"

"Concrete, sweetheart, need to pour today, so if we have to run over one of them on Saturday, then no big deal."

"You're planning on mixing concrete this afternoon?"

"No, ma'am. I've got a buddy who's bringing his truck after his last pour." He glanced at the sun. "We've got another hour or so."

"I suppose he wants cash."

"Cash is always good."

"When did you arrange all this?"

"Yesterday afternoon. Stopped by his place on the way home."

"What if..."

He held his hands up. "He's got one of those mix-on-sight trucks. I figure we wouldn't need more than two yards; he charges a premium, but there's no waste. That's a plus. Besides, we're on his way home."

"But Samuel..."

"So, he's waving the delivery charge if we can get ready. Just trying to save you some money, babe."

"Cool, I do like that part. What can I do to help? I'm no good at using that nasty digger of yours. Surely I can be more productive on another assignment."

"You can pull my truck around back and drop the smoker, then we need three pieces of rebar for each hole, the shorter ones, a little more than waist high so we can knock them down to about two inches below grade."

She pulled his truck around to the back, thanking God above he didn't expect her to do any fancy backing. She hopped out and walked to the back. She climbed up on the trailer and put her shoulder to the still warm grill.

Couldn't budge the thing. She raised her voice to carry above the steady ground pounding. "Samuel?'

The thumping stopped. "Yeah?"

"I can't budge this grill an inch. I don't think I can get it off the trailer by myself."

"I couldn't either, it's welded to it." He chuckled. "Just unhitch the trailer. It's easy. Use the jack." He went back to his digging, verified by the smacking of black dirt.

She walked around and looked at where the trailer rested on the thing sticking out past his bumper with two hookie chains on both sides. The heavy wide hooks weren't easy, and she had to Praise the Lord when she broke a nail to the quick.

Managed to get them off though. Once they lay successfully on the ground, she went to trying to lift the trailer's head dealie off the bumper.

"Hey! Who do you think I am, Superman?"

The digging stopped again. "What?"

"I can't lift this trailer an inch."

"I'm coming." He came into view, shaking his head at her. "Out of the way, Clark Kent." He raised the lever and cranked it around and around and it made a footie deal push against the ground and the trailer rose up and up until it was higher than the little ball. "There you go."

"Smarty britches."

"Now pull my pickup on up from under it and park around front. Be sure you aren't in reverse. The steel is in back."

She gave him her best wrinkled nose, puckered-lips smirk. "Just to be sure, you're talking about those ribbed metal poles about this big around?" She held out a finger.

"Yes, ma'am."

She hopped back into the truck. By the time she got around front, he'd already returned to his emptying the pier holes of their dirt. She parked close as she could and pulled three of the rebar sticks from the truck's bed.

Wow, they were heavy. She'd be making lots of trips! They kept banging either her or the ground, about wore her totally out.

Praise God though, they used to be way longer.

How'd he know about all this stuff?

"Hey, Baylor, when did you cut this rebar?"

✝ ♥ ♫♪ •*•♪♫ ✝

Samuel tapped the digger's tips on his second piece of scrap two-by-four then faced her. "This morning. I had some extra from the last barn we built, so I saved you some dollars." Her using his last name was a good sign.

From back in the days she only called him Baylor whenever she wanted to play, a vision of rough housing with her flashed across his mind's eye, but he blinked it away as fast as he could. He dared not watch another second.

Oh, Lord, keep me on the path You've chosen for me, strengthen me to walk the way You've led me all these years. With her here... You know my needs, Father. I ask in Jesus' name.

He returned to his hole, that one and two more, then he could help her with the rebar. All he needed was for that truck to arrive before he got everything ready.

She walked by on her twenty-somethingth trip to the truck and punched his shoulder. "Ever been close?"

He ignored the invitation to stop working. "Close to what?"

"Oh my goodness, getting hitched, silly."

He raised the digger handles high then slammed them downward. "Not really. Met a few nice ladies along the way, a couple I thought might work out, but none of them did."

"Anyone I'd remember?"

"Don't think so. How about you? Get close?"

She trudged by again dragging three sticks of rebar, headed for the next hole. She dropped the trio in, a few more and she'd be caught up with him. "No. That one ready? Should I start pounding them in?"

He pulled his tape measure off his pants pocket and measured the hole. "A few more inches, won't be long. Knocking them in will be good. Make like a triangle in the middle and pound then about three inches apart to where they'll stand up straight."

Beyond tuckered, it took him a lot longer on the last two, then he joined her getting the steel into the ground in the thirty-three holes.

When the truck arrived, all was ready. He couldn't know how, but some way, he found the strength to fill the holes with mud and tamp it all down nice and snug. She handed over the cash.

Once he directed his bud's backup and the man was gone, he strolled to her sedan where she'd been sitting after paying for the concrete. "Real good day, boss. What time tomorrow?"

"What time's Chucky coming?"

"Six."

"What do we still need to do?"

"Cut down four or five trees, trim a half dozen more, not a lot."

"Want to sleep in?"

"No, but if you do, we should be able to get it all done starting at noon. You'll get the half-day rate."

"Cool, so what are you going to do in the morning?"

"Oh, there's a heifer I haven't seen in a couple of days. Figured if she's not up this evening, I'll go look for her."

"Need any help?"

He smiled. "Been on a horse lately?"

"No, but I'm sure I can still ride."

"First light comes pretty early this time of the year."

She gave him her best fake smile. "I'll be there. You just have the horses saddled. I'll give you the half-day wrangler rate."

"Yes, boss, anything else?"

"Want your money now?"

"You paying me off, sending me home?"

"No, silly, but I've got it now. That concrete wasn't nearly as much as I expected. Guess the way you've been spending my money lately, it may be a good idea to get it while you can. Might run out before too much longer."

"You do know we're just getting started, and it's going to take a lot more than you've spent so far, right?"

She nodded. "I know. I'm gone. See you at first light."

He backed up a step and watched her drive away. *Oh, Lord... Well, it's out there. Has she kept herself pure? Is she the one? Or am I being tested?*

✝ ♥ ♫♪ Chapter Seven

The next morning, much to her surprise, Mary Esther woke before her phone's rooster crowed. She hated that bird. Rolling out of bed, she ignored her aching shoulders, flipped on the coffee, and went about getting herself ready for the day.

In her tummy, she got giddier with each task she accomplished. Visiting a dude ranch once, and another time at a friend's, she'd ridden a few times since she left but…was it riding with Samuel that excited her so?

How could it not be?

She hated leaving him every evening and could hardly wait to see him in the mornings.

But what about her mother? And Ralph?

Halfway to English, she pulled over, Googled the little community, and reinforced what she remembered. Still, driving in the dark without any landmarks threw her off. It'd been so long.

Then she rounded a corner, and his same old big-mouthed bass mailbox sat in its same old place just past the drive with the same old metal corner poles with BAYLOR cut out in steel hanging over the entrance.

She rolled across the cattle guard, her headlights illuminating the old farm house, but no sign of life, no truck or anything. She eased on around to a new metal barn. A travel trailer sat beside it.

When did he get those? The man himself leaned against his truck. Two saddled horses stood ready, tied on either side of the tailgate.

She rolled down her window. "Where should I park?"

He shrugged. "Right there's fine."

She got out, but instead of hugging him hello, she curtsied and held out two fists of skirt like a square dancer dosie-do-ing then raised her skirt a bit to reveal her jeans and boots. "This work?"

"Yes, ma'am, just fine. I didn't think about wearing your wranglers under a skirt, but makes sense." He nodded toward the horses. "You ready?"

She glanced to the east. "Shouldn't we wait for a bit more light?"

"We can. There's coffee in the barn, should still be hot. I just now turned it off."

She followed him in. Two tractors rested on the far left side, three stalls filled the right. He opened the door to what looked to be his tack room or maybe storage. "When did you build this huge new barn?"

"PawPaw and I threw it up the summer before he went home."

"Nice, but I loved the old one."

"I did, too, but we sold its wood for enough to buy the material for the new one." He extended a cup.

She took it. "Wow, who'd think it?"

"That's what we thought."

"So, shifting gears a bit, there's something I need to know."

"Okay."

"Well, Ralph, the man my mother married, we all thought he was a Christian, I mean, he went to church with us every Sunday, but…" She grimaced. "Anyway, suffice it to say, he isn't. At least that's mine and Mimi's theory. And as far as Mother, well –"

"Who's Mimi?"

"Mother's mother."

"Did I ever meet her?"

"Well, she was at the funeral, but she hardly ever came up here. We always went there to visit."

"So exactly what did you need to know?"

She filled her lungs. If it disqualified her, best know now, but if he was so pigheaded….

He put his hand on her forearm. "Mary Esther, what is it?"

The warmth from his fingers spread to her heart. How could it? She was the virgin daughter of the most Godly man she'd ever known. "Hey, it's getting light. Hadn't we best get after it?"

He turned around then looked back. "If you're ready."

She was such a coward. Why couldn't she just spit it out? If he was half as good at relationships as everything else, he should be able to see that she was in love with him, and had been for twenty-six years.

Wow, that long?

What a deal, getting kicked out of kindergarten right into his first grade class.

Not exactly like riding a bicycle, but close. Being there was so right, sitting a horse next to him, especially when the little darlings got close enough for her leg to bump against his. It couldn't matter about Ralph, he didn't raise her.

She barely knew the man. Was it some spiritual thing he'd found in the Bible? Why did she have to be the daughter of God-fearing parents? What was that all about?

"Those ladies you thought might lead to marriage, what happened there?"

"Mercy, girl, you sure are nosey."

"Hey, we've been a whole minute without any conversation, and hey, inquiring minds want to know."

"Nothing happened; they never even knew I was interested."

"How does that work? You didn't go out with them?"

"Heavens no."

"Okay, Baylor, explain yourself because you certainly are not making any sense."

✝ ♥ ♫♪ •*•♪ ♫ ✝

Why was she doing this?

Samuel glanced at her but was unable to get any kind of hint as to exactly what she was after. If she did meet all his requirements, wouldn't she just say so? A dozen scenarios flooded his heart, and he hated everyone one.

Oh, Lord, give me wisdom and understanding. Why did You bring her back into my life?

"Hey, are you going to explain yourself or not?"

"Mary Esther, it's simple enough. If a young lady caught my eye for whatever reason, first of all, I'd pray about it. The Lord eliminated a lot of them, then, well…"

"Those are the ones I want to hear about."

"After a while, if I was still interested, I'd go to her church whenever I wasn't committed somewhere else."

"You church hopped?"

"No. I'm not an official member of any of them." He reined his horse sideways, leaned over and opened a gate, nodded for her to ride through, then closed it. He joined her. "I go wherever I'm invited to teach or preach, otherwise, I have several favorites."

"Ah so, I get it, so you'd visit her church. Then what?"

"Nothing. Never got to the courting stage with any of them."

"Courting? Is that what you call it? How old school is that, Samuel Baylor?"

Both names. She didn't do that much. At least it wasn't the whole package; the only time anyone threw in the Levi, either he'd found trouble or had legal business. Did she even remember his full name?

A rather large blur of black pulled his attention from his musings. "Over there." He pointed toward a cluster of cedars. "Go to the right." He reined left.

Like she'd been helping him work cows all her life, the wayward heifer trotted back toward her herd in maybe record time.

Oh, Lord, if she isn't pure, take her out of my life or take mine. You let David have Bathsheba. Poor baby though, he didn't get to live. Not my will, but Yours, Father.

That's what he was supposed to say, though it sure seemed twenty years without her should be enough. He opened the gate. The yearling darted through as though embarrassed and repentant for getting herself separated.

He closed and tied off the gate then smiled at Mary Esther. "Been cowboying long?"

"Smart aleck. The horse did it all, but you already knew that. I only had to hang on."

"He's a good one alright. Remember that strawberry gray you always claimed was yours?"

"Of course, how could I forget my Bliss?"

"That's her grandson."

"Oh, cool. That's so awesome. So what's this guy's name?"

"Shooter."

"Wasn't that the first Levi Baylor's horse's name?"

"Yes ma'am, at least according to May Meriwether's The Granger novel. But you've got a great memory. It was. Didn't think you'd remember."

"How could you think I'd forget? Besides, I've read all her books more than once. She was way ahead of all her contemporaries. Still, those days as kids…some of the best times of my life."

Exactly, seemed like the last twenty years melted away with the morning mist, and he was twelve again. Except he wasn't, and he had been given a vision. God placed a call on his life. How much easier and more enjoyable would it be with her at his side?

"Hey, Mary Esther, what's your plan?"

"Thought cutting down some trees after dinner—with you."

"No, don't mean today—once you get your house right. Then what?"

"Oh, I don't know, get a job I guess."

"Going back on the road?"

"I don't think so. It definitely fell way short of what I expected. I mean, I love to sing more than anything, especially when it glorifies God, but I don't know." She sighed. "Glad He does." She stretched and yawned.

"You have to get up too early? Need a nap already?"

"I don't take naps, and maybe I didn't get enough sleep. Can't seem to get used to that mattress. It's harder than I like." She shook her head then nodded toward his trailer. "You travel much?"

"Not at all, well, not with that." He swung out of the saddle, opened the home gate and held it for her, then locked it back.

"What's the story on your Silver Streak then? Why'd you buy it?"

He walked along next to her toward his truck. "I didn't. Traded a real nice bull for her. The house doesn't have any insulation, and the floor…" He tied his reins to the back of his truck. "Anyway, it's my bunkhouse now."

She dismounted then followed suit. "You live in it? Rather small. You don't live in your house at all?"

"It isn't too bad. I'm not there much."

"Why don't you fix up the house?"

"I don't think it's worth the effort or the buckage it'd take. Figure I'll take it down one of these days, use as much of it as possible in a new one."

"Oh, I want the porch. We spent so many summer days there. Remember? I wonder how many monopoly games we played on that porch. Sure would be fun to have it on my house. I mean the exact same one."

How could he forget those days and all the games she beat him at? Always maneuvered herself into having the most property with her one-sided barter and negotiation skills, and he never could refuse her.

He put the stirrup over the horn, untied the girth strap, unbuckled the breast pieces, then pulled the saddle off. "That'd be fun, wouldn't it? Let me think on it."

"You're going to think I'm such a weakling, but this strap is too tight, and I can't undo it. I need your help again."

"Be right there."

First, he put his saddle on the tree in the tack room, then took hers off then put it up. Yep, just like when he was twelve. She never had the hand strength then either. Once back, he handed her a brush then went to work on getting his mount ready to turn out.

"Hey, Shooter, I loved your grandame." She started up on his neck, brushing his jaw and giving his forehead a playful swipe, too. "She was my horse. You want to be my horse, too?"

She glanced over at him with a twinkle in her eye. The woman was still the girl, and still such a tease. And he loved her teasing now as much as then.

"You thinking of rustling my horse?"

"He can still live here." From his shoulder she brushed down his leg, careful to go all the way around. She always groomed every square inch. "For now anyway."

With that chore behind him, and when she finally finished, he led both horses through the home gate and pulled the last bridle off. He waved the two geldings away, and they took off, twisting and bucking and having all sorts of fun.

She laughed.

Oh, how he loved the sound of her laughter. Might have been what made him fall so deeply in love with her way back when.

Turning, he faced her. "Talked to my neighbor last night. We'd like to roll your hay."

"Oh really? I've got hay, huh? Guess you can roll it if you want. How does that work?"

He nodded toward the barn. "We do all the work and fertilizing, and give you three, five, then seven dollars a roll if we can get a third cutting out of it."

"Hey, I like the sound of that." She fell in beside him. "Why is there a difference in what I get?"

"Weeds and brush. First cutting has all that, then with fertilizer and rain, the second and third cuttings are better, higher in protein."

"Oh, that makes sense. Sure. Great. It'll be found money for me, and thanks for thinking of it."

"You're welcome. Cobb and I always need hay."

"They stay hungry all winter, huh?"

"Yes, ma'am. And to save you some cash, keep track of my wages, and we can settle up after the last cutting."

"You serious? You don't need it now? I mean, along the way?"

"Naw, I'm a cheap keep. I'm fine right now."

"If you're sure.... "

"I can always tap into my hay money if I need to."

"So you've got a separate fund for hay?"

"Yes, ma'am. Whenever I take calves to the sale barn, I put back enough for the next six months of hay and cubes."

✞♥♫♪ •*•♪♫✞

Mary Esther didn't ask what a cube was, had to be something his cows needed. She couldn't believe it; the man had it going on.

Hard working, levelheaded, taking good care of his herd, and preaching and teaching the gospel; he was certainly blessed.

"What are you doing still here in Red River County? Mercy, Samuel Levi Baylor, you're wasting your God-given talents."

He opened her car door. "What are you talking about? This is my home." He grinned. "So you remembered my middle name."

"What are you saying? Why do you keep thinking I can't remember anything? I did get promoted out of kindergarten after only two weeks to first grade because of my brains. Did you forget that?"

His eyebrows hiked higher, but he only shook his head, didn't say anything.

"Of course I remember your name and my horse and the first twelve years of my life in Clarksville. But really, you have so much to offer. I mean, take Wednesday night. How many were there?"

"Didn't count."

"Fifteen people maybe? You could be preaching to thousands in the Metroplex. Once word got out, you'd be packing them in. Forget live, I have some friends in production, and they'd –"

"No, Mary Esther."

"Hey, my friends would love me for putting them in touch with you. In no time, you'd be doing great on TV. Charismatic as you are."

"Who wants to be on the tube when there's all this instead?" He held out his arms out. "I love it here, the place and the people."

"You could keep all this, and still get them to syndicate a show; you'd be hauling in sacks full of money in no time."

"No, that isn't me."

"Why not?"

He shook his head and looked away.

She walked around him and looked into his eyes, but couldn't get any kind of good read. "What is it, Samuel?"

"A long time ago… Well, the Lord told me never to go on Christian television and not to merchandise the gospel."

"Wow, why?"

"He gave me a vision and a gift and well…"

"Well what?"

"I've never taken a dime for teaching or preaching. And I never will."

"I don't understand why He'd tell you that when His Word clearly says a workman is worth his hire, and not to muzzle the oxen."

"I know what it says, but I do get paid. My wages come straight from the Lord Himself. Long as I trust God to supply all my needs, then…" He spread both arms wide and turned a full circle that time. "He's given me all this, debt free. I don't owe a red cent to anyone. And now…"

"Now what?"

He grinned. "Now you, you're here, home. He's sent me my best friend."

Tears welled, but then Ralph and his heathen self dried them almost as quick. Samuel probably knew she didn't qualify. He'd elevated her from sister to friend, but he sure didn't put a girl in front of it.

Oh, Lord, why did Daddy have to die?

Chapter Eight ✝♥♫♪

As Mary Esther followed him from English to her place, two words swirled across heart—sister and friend. Why did he think of her that way? No wonder she'd never found Mister Right. Who could compare with Samuel?

Apparently, he set the standard she'd been measuring all the others against, without even knowing it.

The pre-teen boy, the best friend she'd ever had in her life—she knew that now—had grown into a wonderful man, a God-fearing man, her completion.

Then another thought pushed out the other.

What if he was holding a grudge?

Of course, that had to be it.

But how?

Only a pigheaded blind man would hang onto something that happened twenty years ago, and everything she'd seen of him belied that. Still, the worst thing a female could ever do was hurt a male's pride.

Though the offense actually happened two decades ago, if you threw out the time she'd been gone, he might consider it as fresh as last week.

If only he had written, she might never have lost touch with him. She could have apologized even if he should be the one to say sorry first. But all the blame shouldn't be at his feet. If it mattered so much, why hadn't she reached out to him?

Pride, such an ugly sin—his and hers. Whether the stolen kiss or the slap, it obviously hurt bad enough to doom communication. But what did it wound? His pride. Her pride.

And forget computer technology or any social medias. He grew up with PawPaw, a stubborn old man who taught him the world-wide web epitomized evil. How many times over the years had she gone to Facebook and searched for Samuel Levi Baylor?

Oh, if it had meant so much, she could have driven.

Should have come in person, actually faced him, and said all the things she wanted to tell him. But no, too wrapped up in her singing, her all-consuming career, she'd never even thought about going. That made it even worse.

Selfish pride!

As much as she wanted him to apologize, even now, she also wanted him to kiss her again, ten times more or a hundred. But somewhere more private, and a time when grief hadn't darkened her heart.

Could that one day so long ago, his stupid kiss or her one little slap, have ruined any chance of her walking the aisle toward him, standing there all decked out in....

Wait. Would she want him in a tux?

She'd earned the right to wear white, not that a lot of girls didn't wear the color of purity anyway. Daydreaming of her wedding day through the years, she always wore a beautiful beaded gown with her groom in traditional formal wear.

But truth be told, she couldn't see Samuel willing to don such froo froo apparel.

Besides, costs would be so prohibitive for a fancy wedding these days. Could she afford it? Her mother or Mimi didn't have any extra dollars. Selling a few acres would pay for a big ceremony, but she'd never do that.

A simple 'I do' in a justice of the peace's office somewhere would work. All the days after were the ones that counted.

Then again, he could sell some cows. Wasn't that what he raised them for? To sell?

But another idea hit her, a brilliant one. It had to be the Lord.

Samuel stopped short of the turn into the woods that guarded where her house would soon rest, got out, and went to working on something in the back of his truck. She joined him. He filled his chainsaw with oil. He owned everything she needed and wasn't even charging her any extra for the use of his tools.

And what about that steel he brought yesterday?

"Hey, I've got an idea."

He looked up. "Okay."

"How about us doing a duet?'

"You know I don't sing."

"Well, I first thought of something like we did last night, but well, would that fall into merchandising the gospel? Even though it might get like a million folks saved. Anyway, before I joined up with Brad and Bev, I sang a little country, still know a few folks."

He pulled the saw out of the truck. "I like country music, some of it anyway. What do you have in mind?"

"By the way, what little you sang Wednesday night—echoing 'He arose'—was right on key, and mercy, Samuel, you have some fabulous pipes."

He left the chainsaw at his side and held up his free hand. "Wait. Are you wanting me to sing with you?"

"No, silly, we can do like we did the other night. You talk, and I'll sing."

"Oh, okay then. What song?"

"Don't know yet, haven't got that far, but I'll make some calls and find out where the closest recording studio is."

"You're serious?"

"You bet I am! Haven't you been listening? Don't you think it's an awesome idea?"

"Well, I suppose, but I figured... I don't know... Guess I thought you were talking about maybe some fun thing we could do on a rainy afternoon. Not recording anything."

"Have you got all the cows you want?"

"No, but...."

She waved him off. Her pulse pounded, and a vision of him and her standing in front of a microphone danced across her mind's stage. "Look, my dear friend, we could be talking a whole bunch of the little moo moo darlings and all the hay and—what are those little square bites again? —those cows would ever need."

"Range cubes." He held up his pointer finger and put his thumb on his second joint. "They're compressed grains and high protein grasses to make solid cubes about this long and twice as fat."

"Yes, sir, that's them."

"We drop them out in a long row on the ground from a truck. It's a sight how they line up in order and go to eating."

"What kind of order? You train them?"

"Not me. They decide. The top cow, usually the meanest, eats first, then right on down, and if Old Boss Mama eats fast enough, she'll run down to get the last cow's, too. So there's a lot of money in recording a song?"

"Absolutely. What do you think is paying for moving and remodeling my house? If it gets radio play time, iTunes' sales go crazy."

"Okay, well, I've never heard of iTunes, but right now, we best get after it."

"Sure, just tell me what you want me to do."

"I'll cut, you drag."

"Drag what where?"

"Limbs and branches. Don't worry with the big ones; I'll cut those up later." He looked around then pointed at the farm field. "Stack it up there in that little hollow. We'll burn it when it dries out."

She looked to where he pointed then turned back, started to protest, but he already had his chainsaw running. Well, she could tell him later, but no way would she allow him to burn anything out in her field.

He'd catch the world on fire.

Besides, she didn't want to see a huge big black spot every time she drove home.

The sapling cedars, oaks, and elms went fast, but then he pulled out a ladder and went to working on trimming the big oak that guarded the entrance. It about did her in. Yeah, wait until the next trip to Big Woods.

It was him working her like a dog, not the other way around. Back and forth, back and forth she dragged the wood, and her pile grew.

The remembrance of that night at the little church swept over her. Mercy, Lord, I want more. A warm fuzziness engulfed her. When had she enjoyed singing a song as much as she did at Big Woods?

How long had it been?

Throwing another arm-sized limb onto her pile, an idea struck her. All of it would make great firewood. She could either sell it or...add a fireplace to the house. Oh wow, she'd love that.

In the hours cuddled with Mimi, watching the flickering flames and glowing embers, she'd told herself more than once when she grew up, she'd have herself a fireplace. From that remembrance, she imagined snuggling in with the love of her life.

The rumbling stopped. He climbed down the ladder and set the saw sideways on the ground. "How does iTunes work?"

Took her longer than she would have guessed to explain people bought music there, but not records or CDs. Digital, electronic. She'd never thought so much about it herself, but finally a light came on in his thick skull.

"So they buy air songs. How much does a sound studio cost?"

She shook her head. "I'm not sure there's any set fees. Different places, you know. It's usually by the hour though. I never was on the money end of it, but not a whole lot if you're in and out."

"Would it take more than a thousand dollars?"

"Oh, no, I don't think so. Couple of hundred maybe, why? What are you thinking?"

"Let's do it. Who do we call?"

"I'd really love to be in your handsome head, Samuel, but I'm not. Explain yourself. Do what exactly?"

"The song we did at Big Woods. Record it and put it on iTunes."

"Woo hoo! Great! Why'd you change your mind? I mean about merchandizing the Gospel?"

"I didn't. I want to give it away. I'll pay for everything."

"What? Why?"

"You said it yourself, millions might be saved, but if we can reach just one person, it'll be worth it."

Give it away? Was he crazy? But his reasoning definitely made sense. She couldn't deny that. "Yes, it would "

"Where's your phone?"

"In my car."

"How about you go to calling, and I'll get back to work?"

Plenty past ready to sit down, she didn't comment on the usefulness of her cell, but then another thought hit her. Adding a phone to her plan wouldn't be that much. He should be in touch. What if she needed him?

She chuckled on the way to her car. Well, of course she needed him. Wanted him bad, the desire to belong to him often overwhelmed her.

Had she been saving herself for him all those years? A part of her must have known. The Lord certainly must have.

I FORMED YOU IN YOUR MOTHER'S WOMB TO COMPLETE HIM

She stopped in her tracks. Oh wow. The voice of the Lord reverberated in her spirit. "Father? Was that you?" She listened. Her heart beat a rhythm that would win a battle of the bands.

Samuel's saw felled another limb that crashed to the ground. Had she heard the words with her ears? It seemed so.

Searching above, she swallowed. The leafless trees' limbs etched stark patterns against the blue sky, and a lazy hawk soared on the scant breeze that swayed only the smallest branches way up high.

The words...so definite. It had to be the Lord. Wow. Hesitant, she started walking again, reliving the Voice and His message to her.

Oh, Lord, get through that thick skull of his and...have him say he's sorry...for what? That he never wrote? Stole that kiss? It's me. Isn't it? Oh, Abba! I repent. I'm so sorry for my stubborn pride. Those things don't matter. They're so trivial. Forgive me, Lord, and tell me what You want me to do. I love You, I praise You and adore You. Thank you, Lord.

Glory bumps rose on her arms and legs.

Could it be true? Did it mean Samuel would be hers?

Mercy! She shook her head and went to fishing in her purse then slid her cell to life and focused on the task at hand.

✞ ♥ ♫♪ •*•♪ ♫ ✞

Samuel stepped back, studying the opening. She should go. He visualized the house making the turn, saw no problem in his mind's eye, but the doing would tell the tale. He glanced west. Had at least another hour, maybe more, before Chucky returned.

He loved hunting hog but wasn't sure about having Mary Esther along.

Hopefully, she'd stay in the Gator and not want to be in on the catch. He rubbed his thigh. The gash had long healed, but he still remembered that boar's tusk slicing his leg. How could he ever forget forty-seven stitches? He looked up.

Mercy, Lord, thank you for keeping me alive that night.

"Next Monday, one o'clock sharp."

He turned toward her. "What happens? What are you talking about?"

"I booked us a sound studio. Our time starts at one, so we need to be there at noon or so. Do we want any backup?"

"Monday afternoon will work. What kind of backup?"

"Singers, maybe a band, I don't know. Or we can get it recorded then have someone mix in whatever we want. I mean, if you happen to know a couple of ladies who could sing backup... but whatever. We need to get to rehearsing. I guarantee you that Monday will be here before we know it."

"No."

"No? Now what are you talking what? I already booked it, gave the man my card number; it's going to cost me –"

He held his hand out. Surprising him, she immediately stopped mid-sentence. She had changed some. Back when, she'd have gone on for at least two more paragraphs. "We will be there on time and will record our song. Maybe more than one, but no rehearsing."

"Well now, that's just crazy. No rehearsing? You don't know what you're talking about. I've been in this business. Time is money, and if we don't have it down cold when we walk into that studio, then we'll be doing take after take trying to get it right."

He stifled a snicker, closed his eyes.

Mercy, Lord, such passion.

He smiled, lowered his voice. "Sweet lady, think Big Woods. We didn't rehearse anything last Wednesday, and it was awesome. You know it was and said so yourself."

"You're right."

"It's been my experience the anointing diminishes proportionately the more we try to put ourselves into what He wants to do. For sure, we do not want to record stale manna."

For a few beats of his heart, fear swelled her eyes, then her pursed lips turned into a weak smile. "It's your dime, so you get to call the plays, but if we run over, don't blame me."

He took both of her hands into his. Oh, how he wanted to pull her in and smother her with kisses, assure her it would be glorious, but holding her hands was bad enough. "It will be great." He backed up a step.

"Hope so."

"Now come look, see what you think." He released one hand, turned, and pulled her to a spot off the road a few feet then nodded south. "I think it's wide enough, what about you?"

Her countenance fell. Giving his hand a little squeeze, she shook her head. "I don't know. It seemed wide enough before, but… Wow, you sure cut down a lot of trees."

"Had to. Making this turn is going to be tricky. They were barely saplings anyway, they'll grow back. Besides, you're tucked into a forest here."

She nodded. "Well, just as long as we don't hurt any of the big ones. They were here when daddy was a boy."

"I agree." He nodded toward his right. "I'd say that old boy is at least a couple of centuries old."

"Really? You think two hundred years? Wow, so it would have been here when your Texas Ranger namesake was?"

"Yes, ma'am, may be even older."

"Okay, so do you figure we're ready then?"

"I do, won't really know until tomorrow, but it sure looks good to me. We can ask Chucky what he thinks." He started back around to where the truck sat. Walking hand in hand seemed as natural as the birds singing overhead.

"Speaking of your friend, want to help me Sunday?"

"Can't. I'm filling in at Cuthand Methodist."

"Sunday morning? What time?"

"Class at ten, worship at eleven."

"Think I could put Chucky off a week?"

He shook his head. "His mother is a Red Hatter, and I'm sure she's got all her friend ladies coming, and I don't think you should. You gave your word you'd be there, remember?"

"Of course I do, but one Sunday seems just as good as another. I mean it isn't like they're pay –" She pulled her hand away and waved him off. "You keep forgetting I was too smart for kindergarten, went straight into first grade. You do remember that, right? How smart I am?"

How could he not recall the day the beautiful love of his life walked in and took the seat right next to him?

"And so humble."

✞♥♫♪ Chapter Nine

Mary Esther resisted the impulse to respond to his sarcasm with something snarky. "You're right. I gave my word. So are you just doing the morning service?"

"No, both."

"How do I get there?"

"You know where the Cross Arrow is?"

"Well, it's south of here, right? On the way to Boxelder? If it's the place I'm thinking, but I didn't drive all over the county when I was twelve—like some people I know."

"That's the one, and it is that direction, except you don't get near Boxelder because at the top of the hill at their big hay barn, you turn right on FM 1423."

She squinted, trying to see the route in her mind's eye.

"Need me to draw you a map?"

Had she looked confused? "Don't bother, I can Google it."

"I've heard people say that. What's googling?"

She bit her lip to keep from smirking. How could he be so electronically challenged? "It's an internet search engine where you can look up anything you'd ever want to know and get the answer with a few taps. All I have to do is type in Cuthand Methodist, and it'll know right where I am and map me out the best route."

"You don't say."

"But yes, I do. It's really amazing. I can't believe you don't have one."

He grinned. "Well, believe it. I've lived thirty-two years without any new-fangled gadgets." He leaned against the truck and crossed his arms over his broad chest. "Get there quick as you can, it's covered dish Sunday."

"Cool." Or was it? She liked her jeans fitting so loose, even if they were under her new skirt. Dinners on the grounds were always so tempting. Mercy, no one cooked as good as bona fide country church ladies.

"And speaking of cool? It's liable to get pretty chilly after the sun goes down. Bring a jacket?" He looked westward; she followed his gaze, but saw nothing.

"I did. At some point, you're going to have to admit I have a head on my shoulders, Samuel Baylor."

"It's getting late." He hiked his eyebrows at her. "We best get on over to the house. Chucky should there any minute."

She pulled out her cell. A quarter 'til six. "So, what? You tell time by the sun? Can't give in to no new-fangled watch?"

"Kept breaking them. Don't need one anyway. PawPaw's truck's got a clock, and there's two or three in my trailer." He nodded toward the north. "Come on, let's go."

She marched on to her car. Yes, he needed a cell whether he knew it or not. Should be able to add one to her plan at Radio Shack on the square. If she could just get him to try it, he'd see how great and useful they were.

Of course, she'd have to make the pigheaded hunk carry it. She chuckled as she eased behind her wheel. Like she could make him do anything.

She'd ask him to write and he'd promised, but no. One little tiny love tap to his cheek and his letter writing hand went numb. Ha! Who was being the pigheaded idiot now? She hurt his heart. Oh, she needed to quit thinking about all that.

No way she could change the past.

God, give me a song to set my mind onto whatsoever is pure and holy and worthy of a good report.

By the time she got back to the house, she had it. She stepped out and walked over to his truck's passenger side and hopped in.

"Listen to this. I will not dwell on any thoughts that are evil. I will resist every word that's negative. I refuse to gossip and complain, and I won't look for someone to blame, when the devil starts to play that rotten game."

Her tone changed from sinister to light and breezy, and she finished her new song. "I choose to think on things that are lovely. I'll concentrate on whatsoever's good. It's by our love that we'll be known. I choose to laugh instead of moan, and thereby honor Him Who waters seeds I've sown."

"I like it." He looked like a bobble head. "That's good."

Him enjoying it made her heart smile.

ASK HIM TO FORGIVE YOU. SWALLOW YOUR PRIDE. BLESSED ARE THE PEACEMAKERS.

Her face heated, and her mouth went dry. She knew the Lord's voice. And His Word was true. She did need to ask for forgiveness. But when?

Give me the right time, Father.

Should she say something right then? But Chucky would be driving up any minute. It wasn't anything she wanted to say with someone there.

And it wasn't like she could just spit it out, and it'd be done either. Surely, it would lead to a conversation, some sort of discussion. Maybe he'd be obliged to spill his guts finally and explain why he never wrote.

Battling with herself, she only half listened to what he was telling her about the hunt. Her heart beat faster, and she knew she had to say it, ask him if he would forgive her. She hated not being immediately obedient when she knew that she knew it was God.

And she did.

Then here came Chucky's truck and trailer bouncing down Farm-to-Market 412. She sighed a big breath of relief. Every muscle in her body—tensed in preparation of her obedience— suddenly relaxed.

Saved by good old Chucky!

Of course she needed to ask him to forgive her, and she would, maybe right after he admitted he shouldn't have kissed her right there in front of everyone, would be the perfect time.

Wow! Samuel's friend pulled a big trailer loaded with a little covered car thing, and a four wheeler in the back of his truck. Excellent, no walking.

Two wire cages held five dogs, all barking and wanting to get out. Four skinny ones in the back with cute floppy ears wore black rubber collars with little antennas. Decked out with a thick leather vest that ended in a ring of one-inch spikes around his neck, the one in the front cage looked dangerous.

Pit bull if she had it right, mean-looking beast.

The men went to work unhooking and unloading what they called the Gator, but according to the manufacturer's logo splashed in several places, in reality John Deere made it. Looked like a cute little toy pickup and she loved its shiny green color and yellow wheel rims.

Her daddy had always been a Deere man.

In like two minutes, they had the Gator off the trailer and sitting by Chucky's truck, dropped the trailer, then put the tailgate down and set two metal ramps. Samuel hopped up into the bed and drove the four wheeler almost straight down the ramps.

Talk about treacherous, she'd never do that. If the thing flipped over, she'd be dead, simple as that. Men!

A little rat terror—er, terrier—not more than five pounds suddenly appeared in front of her, barking and jumping around here to there as though eaten alive by ADD. It too wore an antenna on its collar.

"Awe, shut up, Brutus. Chucky looked at her then the hyper dog. "That's Mama's baby girl. Her real name's Olive, but she's the best scent hound I've got."

"Wow." She didn't close her mouth. "And your mother let's her go hogging? Isn't it hazardous for such a wee girl?"

The man laughed. "She hates it, but the Brute drives her crazy the whole time I'm gone if she doesn't get to go, so here she is."

She pointed to the mean looking pit bull. "What's his name?"

"That's Popeye, hog took one eye out."

Samuel stepped in between her and Chucky. "We ready? Where's your coat, baby?"

Baby. She liked the sound of that, like he was claiming her for his friend's sake. Or maybe just showing off for Mister… "Hey, Chucky, what's your last name? Seems to me someone didn't make proper introductions the other day."

He nodded at her. "Bishop, Charles Goodnight Bishop." He stuck out his hand across Samuel, and she shook it.

"Glad to meet you, Charles."

He waved her off. "Awe, that's my granddad. Call me Chucky or I probably won't remember to answer."

"You've got it."

Soon enough, she rode shotgun on her way to the bottoms. She and Chucky with Olive in his lap in the Gator, Samuel followed beside her on the four-wheeler.

Both men had strapped on heavy leather belts with little chains and leather straps hanging on them. Both guys also had rather large knives in holsters on their hips, but no guns.

Someone should have warned her that no one carried any fire power. She'd Googled pictures and watched a few YouTube videos on hog hunting, and they looked horrible, ugly, and meaner than a horde of mother grizzlies.

And these men intended to, what? Catch them with their bare hands? Oh, dear, they were crazy. Why did males always exhibit the need to risk life and limb?

Neither one of them seemed concerned in the least. They cut up and bantered back and forth with her in the middle. Guess she shouldn't be apprehensive either. But then she had no intention of getting out.

"You should've let me drive, because I am not getting out for the duration."

He laughed real big. "What? Who's gonna jump on the hog's back and hold 'em still while Sammy and I tie 'em up?"

"Not me, I guarantee!"

He cackled. It tickled her that he found that so funny. She leaned back in the seat then looked over at Samuel. Jealousy skewed his handsome face, and she realized he wasn't in on her and Chucky's joke.

She smiled an everything's-alright-sugar grin, but he didn't smile back. Surely it didn't upset him.

He'd called her baby.

She liked that. Life was looking up. She filled her lungs, knowing she could forget him saying anything first. Too pigheaded for any such thing as that. Soon as she had him alone again, she'd ask him to forgive her, then maybe she'd slap him all over again for not writing her.

Mercy, twenty years without her best friend ever, over one silly slap?

Wasn't right.

Across the block of black dirt farm land that her daddy called the middle bottoms, then across a big culvert into the lower bottoms. Chucky stopped and Olive exploded off his lap like an Olympic gymnast. He jumped out and opened the front cage.

The four bigger scent-hounds bounded after the little terrier and went to hunting scent. "Hurry up now, girls. Hurry."

Chucky came around to the passenger side. "You want to drive, scoot on over." He hopped into her place, pulled out a tablet-sized box, and punched it on. He smiled. "Now we wait."

"For what? How do we know when they've found something?"

"You'll see. Never takes the little Brute long."

His condescending tone irritated her, but hey, she'd got his services for half price and she didn't mind earning that other half driving him around on the black land she loved. Since she had no intention of spending a lot more time with him, he could talk to her anyway he wanted. What did she care?

A high-pitched frenzied bark followed by a chorus of bays, pulled her upright. Her pulse quickened. "That's it, isn't it?"

"Yes, ma'am." Chucky pointed south. "Two hundred yards. Hit it."

She stomped the gas. The Gator sprang forward, throwing her and him back. Samuel raced ahead, down a draw then on the other side of a tree island. Right out in the middle of her lower bottom farm field, the dogs circled up, barking and lunging then retreating at a monster ugly black hog. She drove as fast as she dared; didn't want to seem too much like a pansy.

"There. Stop there."

She did, only fifteen feet from the hullabaloo. Samuel opened a side door on the back cage, hooked a chain on the pit bull's collar and held on as Popeye jumped out and headed for the circle.

Chucky moved in and pulled one of the hounds back. Samuel released the pit, and in no time—literally a very few blinks—he'd latched onto the hog's snout. Wow, that was one brave dog!

The dogs' owner grabbed both of the porker's back legs. Oh, dear Lord, why would he do that? He was going to be killed. Then to her horror, Samuel swung his legs over the hog and wrapped a chain around his snout.

Could she believe her eyes? Hardly! She'd come home. Found her love. And now he was about to die right before her eyes.

"Get off! Get back!" She didn't care anymore what they thought. Pansy, petunia, it didn't matter. "Samuel! Samuel Levi Baylor! Get back!"

But by then, Chucky had the back legs wrapped and tied and worked on the front ones. Hog tied, so that's what the old saying meant; truss one up so it couldn't go anywhere. She remembered to breathe. Shook both her hands.

One thing she knew with all certainty, she hated hog hunting.

"Baby, bring that trailer closer."

After her third jackknife, he relieved her of driving duties. She never could back up a trailer. So what if she was a girly girl, not some truck driver? Why learn a skill she'd never use? Wasn't like she couldn't back up her car.

Matter of fact, she could be a professional car backer upper. "What now?"

"We'll hike him up into the cage."

They did, slicker than black dirt mud. They put a rope through the cage then around the boar's neck and tied the other end to the four-wheeler. The beast stunk worse than an outhouse.

Who wanted to breathe through her nose or get close to it? No Mary Esther. Snorting and squealing, the boar charged the cage like crazy. Putting Popeye back into the second cage made it worse.

More high-pitched barks and deep-throated bays sounded in the distance. Chucky pulled out his GPS monitor then jumped on the four-wheeler and headed farther south. Samuel slid into the Gator's driver seat and sped after him.

Once he got the side-by-side going way too fast, he glanced at her. "Having fun?"

"Are you kidding me? No! I hate it, and I'm never coming again."

He tended to his driving then glanced over again. "Me neither."

"Why not? Thought you loved hunting hog."

The barks and bays grew closer instead of answering. He pulled to a stop only a few feet from that hog and dog brawl and went to helping Chucky. Three fair-sized mother pigs squealed and circled up, trying to protect their babies.

Must have been half a dozen or more real cute little piglets. One sow, a filthy dirty pink with spots, split Mary Esther's eardrums with her wailing.

The other two big ones were a reddish brown. Wow, she had no idea they came that way, thought they were all black. Took longer than the first one, but before the last bit of sunlight faded, the men had all the wild swine caged—well, two babies broke ranks and dashed for it, made it into the tree line.

Poor little guys.

Tickled her watching Samuel running around, grabbing the mini-squealers.

Why men willingly subjected themselves to such noise, she did not understand. Still, that last dive her man had made trying to catch the little escapee made the hunt worth it. Like it was his place, he scooted in under the Gator's steering wheel.

"What are you grinning about?"

"You."

"Me? What did I do?"

"Oh, you running around all crazy, grabbing those babies. Can't catch enough to get ahead."

"Whatever." He looked toward Chucky, who sat the four-wheeler way up ahead, then back to her. "Hang on."

Way slower than she wanted, Samuel got her back to the house, but then the dogs were all riding on the outside of the cages, and the Gator was hauling a lot more weight than before.

The stink and the racket from the hogs ramming the cages and the dogs trying to bite the pigs through the wire about did her in. If it hadn't been dark and uphill the whole way, she might have got out and walked.

While the men worked, she retreated to her car; praise God for CDs and windows. Mercy, she'd never ever never do that again, even if Chucky offered to work for free. It wasn't worth it.

Finally, they had everything loaded, except for the four-wheeler and with the trailer already hitched, she figured she could safely assume they planned to leave it there, but why?

With Samuel hot on his bud's heels, they strolled toward her. She rolled down her window. Chucky bent down, his face a bit too close. Samuel took turns glaring at her then him. His friend smiled. "What time in the morning?"

"You tell me?"

"Let's sleep in. Say eight?"

She resisted saying nine. She wanted to get her house moved, and if Samuel thought he needed help... "I'll be here with coffee and donuts."

"Sure, that'll be great." He patted her forearm. "Alright then, see you when the morning comes."

He got in his truck, waved at Samuel on the way by then pulled past her. Instead of the four-wheeler in the truck's bed, he had another cage full of the dogs. Samuel climbed into his truck. Headlights filled her sedan.

Jumping out, she waved him to a stop. Her mouth suddenly went dry. Her heart flipped, skipped, and threatened to beat out of her chest.

Oh, Lord.

"Uh, there's something." Her voice came out all crackled. She cleared her throat. "There's something...."

His face, what little she could see in the dark, went from flint to concern. "What, Mary Esther? What's wrong?"

Her name sounded like music when he said it. "Well..." She hated saying it, but to be obedient....

He opened his door. "Tell me. What's wrong?"

"I'm sorry." Best way was just to rush it out with no explanations, get to the nitty gritty. "Will you please forgive me?"

Mercy, that wasn't so hard, and the weight burdening her spirit lifted. She just might float away.

"Of course, always, but for what?"

"Slapping you."

He studied the ground too long, but was grinning when he looked back up. "Of course, I will. And will you forgive me for trying to kiss you?"

"Trying? Uh, I believe you did the deed."

"You're right. Will you forgive me for kissing you? It was wrong, especially at your daddy's funeral."

"Yes, I will. And I know for a second, I kissed you back, but mercy, Samuel, my whole family was there—all around—what if someone saw us?"

"There's no excuse for my behavior. I know that, but you were leaving. I didn't know if I'd ever have another chance." He smiled. "So you kissed me back? All I remembered was that nasty swarm of bees that stung my cheek."

"Probably hurt my hand as much as it did your face, and yes. I kissed you back."

"So are we good, then?"

"Not quite right. Not yet. As long as we're talking about those days, why didn't you write me? You promised."

"I did, more than once, and you sent them all back, marked address unknown like that Elvis song."

"No siree! I did no such thing. You never wrote!" Her volume and tone surprised her.

He held both palms toward her and backed toward his truck a step. "Hold it right there, little missy. I'll see you in the morning, and we can settle this then."

"But you're accusing me of something I never did."

He hopped into his truck, started it up, and drove off without another word.

Well, she never.

Chapter Ten ✞ ♥ ♫♪

In his favorite chair, Samuel sat upright in his miniscule living-dining combination. Her letters still in his lap, he wiped his face, glanced at the clock, and blinked until it registered. Five fifty-five.

Did that mean something? Was God showing him triple grace?

He pushed himself up. Best get after his chores, Chucky would be at her house in two hours.

Setting the bundle aside, he shifted out of sloth mode. Why hadn't he made himself go to bed last night? Well, PawPaw always claimed folks overrated sleep. He grinned, thinking of the old man he still missed every day.

Carrying a steaming mug along, he headed out to feed the stock and his barn cats. He rubbed the back of his one semi-tamed feline. He scratched the dark calico he called Smokey and all the reasons he fell in love with Mary Esther in the first place flooded his soul.

Not one woman had ever come close to comparing.

Oh, Lord, make a way. Tell me what I should do.

Finally, he pulled out and beat her to the job. So had Chucky. But that was good. Early always proved better than late. Then like he and his hog hunting buddy moved a house every day, the morning's work commenced.

Mary Esther arrived ten minutes after the hour, though he would never have known if she hadn't got out apologizing. Guess the money lady could keep her own schedule, come and go as she pleased.

To her credit, she did have a big box of goodies. She pointed to the far end.

"Cherry and chocolate cream-filled. I've got creamer and sugar for the coffee, if anyone wants it."

Chucky stuffed an entire glazed donut in his trap then reached for a pig in the blanket. Samuel enjoyed the look of disdain she gave the man as he wolfed down the food.

But why should he be so jealous? She showed no interest in his friend, and besides, if she wasn't the one as he thought....

He'd about give anything, but she couldn't be.

Quite apparent from her reaction to his list of wife requirements, somewhere, sometime, a hairy-legged scoundrel had caught her fancy. If only he'd been there, or better if her daddy hadn't died.

Mercy, Lord, thank You for bringing her back into my life even if not for a wife. Your Word says a friend is closer than a brother. Reaching folks with the Good News through her music, make that enough. As always, not my will but Yours be done. Help us get that house moved today. In Jesus' name. Amen.

A peace settled over his heart. Maybe it simply wasn't meant to be. Paul never married.

Chucky had brought his deuce and a half to pull the house. After one last inspection of the route, especially the turn, the old girl rolled out. Mary Esther in his truck ahead, lights flashing, him walking behind and to the side to warn Chucky if anything went amiss.

Nothing to it. Until the old house reached the last turn.

His hired help pulled to the right then stopped. His back right set of duels had sunk a good eight inches in the soft dirt.

Samuel met him there. "What do you think?"

"Your truck four-wheel drive?"

"You bet."

"Let's chain him to mine. If I dig a hole, we can forget making this turn today."

Samuel studied on it a minute then shrugged. "We can get Mary Esther to spot us, but I best drive my truck."

He walked around the big diesel and whistled at her, but she didn't move, seemed intent on something in her lap. Oh, Lord, she'd found the letters. Why hadn't he put them in his glove box?

✞ ♥ ♫♪ •*•♪ ♫ ✞

Twenty-six. He'd written her twenty-six letters. The truck door opening jarred Mary Ester out of her trance.

Samuel filled the opening, looking like a little boy with a toad in his pocket. "We need your help."

Tears wet her cheeks. "Why? Why'd you send them to Dallas? Didn't I tell you my Mimi lived in Irving?"

He stared at her a minute, shook his head, then pulled a folded piece of paper from his shirt pocket. Straightening it out, he offered it to her. She immediately recognized her own flowing swirly cursive that had only changed slightly over the last two decades.

And right there in all its failed glory, the address she'd given him all those years ago glared Dallas right before the Texas--and with no zip code. How could she have done that? Why had she ever made such an awful, horrible mistake?

"Oh, Samuel! I'm so sorry. I don't know why I put Dallas instead of Irving. I knew better. I guess I sometimes call the whole Metroplex Dallas, even when I'm in Tarrant County. If I'm going to Colleyville or Grapevine, I call it Dallas, but oh my sweet goodness, I never... Can you forgive me? Will you?"

"Of course. I always thought you were returning them like that old Elvis song. They were always marked address unknown, no such number."

"Hey, you two! Are we gonna get this thang done or not?"

Samuel extended his hand. "Come on, we need your help."

Wiping her cheeks, she took it and let him pull her out. If she could have her druthers, she'd send Chucky home and be alone with Samuel and talk it all out, but that couldn't happen. Not until her home rested on its new foundation in its new woodland location.

Even if most of all, more than anything else, she wanted to read her letters. If they were....

Soon as her feet hit the ground, she leaned in close. "Are they mine? Are you going to let me read them?"

"Yes of course, they're yours to do with as you like. Read them, burn them—"

"Oh, I'd never—"

Chucky stood tight behind Samuel "Hey, you two. I ain't got all day."

"Man, didn't your mama ever tell you patience was a virtue?" He turned back to Mary Esther. "Let's get back to getting your house in place. We can discuss this later."

The hired help snorted. "That's what I'm talking about."

"I don't know how I can help. What is it you need me to do?"

He explained, then the men got everything ready to implement the plan.

First, they chained Samuel's truck to Chucky's front hooks. He positioned her in the very back with instructions to watch the movement of the house and holler a warning of any impending disaster.

Chucky whistled a go, and Samuel eased out, taking the slack from the chain.

His bud gunned his diesel, and the house went into motion again. She rocked a little to the right and Mary Esther started to yell, but she came back level then barely missed a granddaddy oak with her back corner.

Twice, she thought the roof would take out a limb, but Samuel had perfectly trimmed the route—how he knew exactly how high it would be up on that trailer, she had no clue. Sure praised the Lord that he did though.

It made the corner, and her new home headed straight toward its new place a few yards this side of the pool.

The guys hollered back and forth a time or two. Before the end, they got out and went into another inspection consultation. They moved it a few more feet, and voila! It was there. She ran around to the back.

Or at least she thought, but it wasn't. Needed to go back and sideways a little, maybe thirty feet.

Her best friend joined her, grinning ear to ear. "What do you think, boss?"

"Looking good, but I sure can't figure out how y'all are going to get it back into where it needs to go."

"We'll jack her up and take out the wheels then bring them around dead center. That'll be the tricky part. Hook the truck back up and pull her straight into where she goes."

"Oh dear, that's going to be so much hard work, isn't it?"

"Yes, ma'am. That's why I wanted Chucky."

"Well, is there any way you could run me over to my car? If you don't need me that is."

"I can do that. Why though? What are you wanting to do?"

"What do you think?" She grinned. "I want to read my letters. I mean, I'll stay and help if you need me. Don't want to abandon you." Not ever again she told herself, but didn't give it voice.

"Naw, come on. I'll take you." He headed for his truck, hollering over his shoulder. "Hey, Chucky, be right back."

Pulling up behind her car, he stopped. "What about dinner at say, one, since we had a late breakfast?"

"Sure, I can get that. What are you hankering for?"

"A burger, whatever, food's food."

She finished the third letter at twelve twenty-eight and wiped her cheeks, forcing herself to refrain from opening number four, the first un-mailed one. Kind of the same theme, how sorry he was.

Poor little boy. In two and three both, he begged her not to send them back and for her to please write.

She U-turned around the big center tree—It looked so weird without the house there—and hooked 'em to the Dairy Queen for some Hungerbuster combos, and she'd bring them both back a celebratory blizzard.

There and back it took all her will power not to open number four. Three had said he'd not bother her again if it came back, so why did he write the others?

The progress the two men had made surprised her. The desire to get the house in place trumped her passion of reading more letters right then—his long beautiful, sappy letters. She'd hurt him so bad. Reading them now hurt hers.

In a way, they really saddened her heart, thinking of what could have been if only her daddy hadn't died or if Mama wouldn't have moved off to the Metroplex. But the words the Lord had spoken to her spirit rang again.

She would have her happy ending. Wouldn't she?

Whatever pain he'd been carrying all those years without knowing... Wouldn't finding out it had been just a huge misunderstanding—her ghastly mistake—heal his wounds? He had to see that she completed him.

Surely he knew that God created her for him and him for her.

Why, the marriage could be tomorrow!

How much were plane tickets to Vegas? It didn't matter! She didn't want to get married in Sin City.

Monday! He could take her to the courthouse and get a license. Her wheels went to turning fast as an icy day could turn into a balmy seventy degrees in Texas! She could have it all in place by next Sunday.

Bigwoods or Cuthand Methodist, it didn't matter—but not the Church of Christ. How could they have a wedding without music?

She'd be a bride—then married and a wife—and by the next year, a mother.

But reality raised its ugly head and drowned her dreams with a bucket of iced water. She'd totally forgot one very important thing.

He hadn't asked her.

She glared at him while he ate. Willed him to come to his senses. Surely her step-father not being saved... Besides, maybe he was but only backslid. He stood, crumpled his wrapper and shoved it into his empty fries' box.

Then he smiled as though oblivious to her glaring and the subliminal message she'd been trying to send. "We're one gorgeous girl short of a full crew. How about it? Want to volunteer?"

✝ ♥ ♫♪ Chapter Eleven

While he'd eaten, Samuel had noticed her mental wheels turning, caught the glare, but couldn't fathom its root. He smiled. Her reaction to him calling her gorgeous thrilled his heart.

And she was. He'd never known a more beautiful woman, inside or out, but then he'd always been partial.

Mercy, Lord, You made her so desirable.

Could that be it? Did God mean for him to only love her from afar, do what David should have done with Bathsheba?

"Well, well, Mister Flatterer, you know I'm willing to do whatever you need me to, long as you think I'm able. So, tell me. What's your game, and what's my part?"

He laughed. Even if she wasn't meant to be his wife, just being around her… Could it satisfy the longing in his spirit? Would it be enough? Maybe sex was overrated. Maybe he wasn't ever to know, and if that's what God had planned for him….

Obedience was better than sacrifice.

How many more lost souls could he lead to the cross and salvation with her by his side? That could be the purpose.

Chucky set his soda down. "Labor's the game, gofer's the name." He grinned. "Sure would speed things up."

✝ ♥ ♫♪ •*•♪ ♫ ✝

Mary Esther smiled at Samuel then nodded to his friend.

"You got it then. I'm all about speeding up this process." She clapped, rubbed her hands together, clapped twice more, then slapped her thighs, but resisted breaking into song. "We ready?"

The guys seemed too eager, and as though she was a sixteen-year-old boy they wanted to teach a lesson about how real men did things, they worked her. Yeah, that was it.

Like her daddy always said after a long day, he'd been worked hard and put up wet. In theory, she knew what it meant in relation to a horse, but in practice, she'd never experienced any such thing.

Never really dawned on her exactly what hard labor entailed until she got involved with this house moving business. Toting, kneeling, pushing, pulling, walking, jogging; always on the move; lifting, carrying blocks or jacks or getting drinks.

To be certain, one of them always needed something.

Just as the sun slipped below the tree line, the old girl sat readied for her last waltz ever. Mary Esther held her breath as Chucky eased forward. It rocked to the right, she gasped then relaxed a bit when it settled back.

It'd be worse than terrible if it all went wrong now, after all the effort the guys—and she—had put into it.

Samuel held his hands up. "Stop. That's it."

Chucky jumped out. The men eyeballed it from all angles then asked what she thought. It looked good to her, no, much better than good. "Great! It looks great! Even better than I ever imagined. Yahoo! We did it!"

Getting it jacked back up enough to slide the axles out took all the daylight left and better than an hour of burning Coleman lanterns and those little bright flashlight jobbies that clipped onto the bill of their caps.

It tickled her that the guys seemed to have everything, anything they might ever need, right there handy in their trucks.

She leaned against the door of his pickup waiting to turn off the headlights and surveyed the grand accomplishment. She loved her home's new home. Her childhood home was moved, just like she envisioned. Now came the fun and expensive part.

Fishing the cash from her jean skirt pocket, she paid Chucky off and sent him on his way with the promise to be there early at his mother's church in the morning.

Samuel slipped in beside her. "We did it."

She smiled her I-love-you grin. "Yes, sir, we surely did; well, in reality, you did it with a little help. Is there anything you can't do?"

He returned her smile, and in that moment, she knew he loved her, too.

He just had to make a concession for Ralph, especially since the man wasn't really her father. Her real daddy had been the most Christ-like man she'd ever known. He'd pass Samuel's standards with flying colors if only he hadn't...

"Can't carry a tune; and I know absolutely nothing about the internet." He shrugged. "Want me to go on? The list is endless."

"No, not necessary, but some day in the future, I do intend to teach you how to Google at least. You hungry?"

"Sure am, but I need to get on home. Still got chores."

"You up for something spicy? I love Rio Verde's steak Mexican." More than food, she wanted to give him the opportunity to pop the question. She really needed to get going on the wedding. There was so much to do.

"Love the place, it's great." He shook his head. "But I best take a rain check. I'm beat, and your horse gets real testy if he doesn't get to eat close to his regular schedule."

Her heart said make him, insist, but her head knew better. "Okay, sure, I understand. So I'll see you at Cuthand Methodist tomorrow afternoon?"

"Yes, ma'am. I'll be there. Come hungry."

She watched until his truck's taillights disappeared, took one last look at her home resting there in the moonlight, looking perfect, as though that's where it was meant to be all along.

She gazed at the stars—which never failed to astonish her and swell her heart with love for God—and smiled. "You like it, Daddy? I love it!" Coming home was the best thing she'd ever done, bar none.

She hurried to her car then back into town. Since he wasn't coming, she'd forego eating. Twenty-three more letters waited to be read. After a short stop at the McDonalds for a sweet tea, she locked herself in her room-away-from-home.

Piling all the pillows up on one side, she flipped the antique bedside table lamp on, and unfolded letter number four.

April, 17
Dear Mary Esther,
I don't know why you sent my letters back, but just in case you change your mind or come home, figured I'd talk to you a little, tell you what's going on here. Remember the Herreras? They moved, somewhere in Dallas so I asked Jessica to be on the lookout for you, tell you to write or come see me. Sure hope she runs into you.

Be summer before too long, PawPaw said I couldn't take the bus to come look for you, he said Dallas was too big of a place, and I could never find you.

Pulling a Kleenex from the table box, she wiped the blur from her eyes then read on. He was so cute relaying community news and writing so many run-on sentences. She'd always helped him with his English papers.

In return, he'd helped her with history and math. She scanned the old news, catching his sweet innuendos of missing her so much, then at the bottom of the third and final page:

I know I'm only a kid, but I've seen a lot and know about a lot of stuff, and Mary Esther I know this with my whole heart. I love you.

I've loved you from that first day you walked in and sat down next to me in first grade.
Bye for now, hoping you come home soon.
Samuel L. Baylor

She hugged the notebook paper to her heart, and shook her head. If only she'd gotten them. The threat of the tear dam bursting tickled her nose. He loved her. He'd loved her from the first day.

To combat the welling tears, she blinked profusely. Once she could see clearly again, she folded number four and carefully placed it back into its envelope.

After sipping a little Mickey D's sweet tea, and steeling herself as much as possible, she opened number five. She really appreciated him dating them.

August 22
Hey Mary Esther,
    Just got back from a ten state trip with PawPaw, had a blast, but school starts in three days and well its breaking my heart that you'll not be there. I always hope you'll come home and be there.
     Got to go, more later.
    Wow, is seventh grade in Dallas like it is here? We've gone to eight classes and that many different teachers, Coach Jackson, you remember him? He teaches math and is one of my football coaches.
    Hate it that our plans of you being head cheerleader and me star quarterback together are shot, they made me a linebacker on defense and right guard on offense, I like it okay, but it sure would be better if you were here.

She shook her head. Regular school would have been fun, especially in Clarksville with him, but resolved to home school, her mother and Mimi wouldn't take no for an answer. She liked it better than she thought she would.

Guessed it worked out okay. A page and a half of news later, on the fourth page, his words stopped her.

    Jody Reynolds, remember her, she's in eighth grade, but actually younger than me, or I wouldn't even be considering it, she passed me a note in Art yesterday, and I'm not sure what I'm going to do, seventh and eighth have Art together, anyway, she said she'd really like to be my girlfriend, and that you were never coming back.
    Where are you Mary Esther, I miss you so much. Come home please. I still love you. I'll always love you.
    Samuel

She closed her eyes and scanned all the upper class girls, but couldn't picture a Jody. Well, she would've been a year ahead. Okay, he continued professing love. She replaced number five into its envelope, set it aside then gently opened the next, but it was dated four months later.

December 19
Blessings Mary Esther,

Sorry it's been so long sense I've written, but you are five letters behind now, and school and football then basketball and guess time slips by plus PawPaw bought me three mother cows. Their Black Angus, we're keeping track, and I have to pay him back, but the way we figure it, the calves will pay off the mothers in three years, Lord willing, guess what.

I got saved, this real cool preacher came to Clarksville, I thought I was okay with God, but oh, after listening to the man, the Lord went to convicting me, well, I knew and he knew and so did about a dozen other folks, it was great, he stayed late baptizing us all, kind like the Church of Christ, PawPaw said

But anyway how are you and Jesus? I remember you got saved that summer you went to your Mimi's, and she sent you to that camp right, so guess if I don't ever see you again here, we can spend time together in Heaven. I hope you keep reading the bible, I love to

She closed her eyes and thought back to that summer at Mount Lebanon. Though hating being away from him for three whole weeks, she loved getting to go to summer camp. Totally awesome experience.

And he remembered when she gave her heart to the Lord. How precious was that?

He went on for a full page telling her about the revival and all the people who got baptized with him. Said he wanted to be a missionary, but then he'd never left Red River County. She, on the other hand, had no desire to go away across the world to share the love of Christ, didn't want to get that far away from her mother.

Not when she could sing about Him right there.

Speaking of her mother, she should call her and catch her up on the news. Should she tell her about Samuel? Go ahead and just ask about Ralph so she could know for sure if he was still a heathen or not?

Well, it couldn't matter whether he was or not. If Samuel still loved her… He did, didn't he? She sat the phone back down and opened her next letter.

Then another number came to mind; he never mentioned that Jody girl again, slid her phone to life, after nine already, she could ask him tomorrow afternoon about the little hussy.

What was the girl doing telling him Mary Esther wasn't ever coming back? She spread her arms out in a good stretch. Aches and pains shot through every part of her weary self.

"I'm here now, aren't I?" She laughed at herself for being such a ninny over an old imaginary rival.

She picked up number seven and studied the date, shouldn't open that one... Needed to get up early and work on whatever she was going to sing at Chucky's mother's church tomorrow, but….

March 22
Hey Mary Esther,

Been a while, what two years, guess I don't think of you ever day like I used to, but I dreamed about us last night and thought I'd write it down, I hope your staying real close to Jesus, that's so important and well, I really want… Anyway, things have been going good here, how about you? Girl I miss you something awful, do you even remember me? In my dream we made up the very next day, how did you learn to slap so hard, I mean I never got hit as hard in football as you slapped me, or maybe because you were leaving and your dad had died or I don't know, anyway I had a new calf this morning and PawPaw suggested naming her after you I said no, that there was only one of you and well I've tried to not think about you, but I can't. I'm still in love with you.

Hey I've got my driver's licenses now, once I save up enough to get my own truck I'm coming to Dallas to look for you. Needle in a haystack, but with God all things are possible.

Oh they're having a special services this Sunday evening, anyone that wants to preach can have fifteen minutes, I was the first one to sign up, I'm so nervous and excited about it, and even worse the Lord says not to write it down. Sure would be nice to see you sitting there in the front pew.

It's getting late and oh I almost forgot, Jody Reynolds ask me if I'd take her to the Junior Senor Prom, I haven't decided yet, she said she knew she'd have to ask that I'd never say anything and she's right, wow be great if I could take you, wouldn't' everyone be shocked if I waltzed in with my best friend on my arm. I'd have to sell a calf to pay for it but it'd be worth it.

Come home to me Mary Esther, please come home
Samuel Levi Baylor

She grabbed another tissue and dabbed her eyes. Oh, Freddy Fender had it right about wasting days and nights. Why couldn't that Jody girl mind her own business? She simmered a bit then sipped some tea and studied her room.

The mural on one wall in her room really set a good mood. Maybe she'd paint one on that back dining room wall. Well, even if he did go to the prom with the too forward girl, he wanted to take her instead.

She wiped her cheeks and read on.

Oh, you should have been there this past Sunday evening, preaching the good news is so cool, and well hope you don't get mad, but I told Jody I'd take her, bless her heart, I was trying to tell her no, but well she started to cry and then when I said I couldn't afford it, she said her daddy would pay for everything and well mercy Mary Esther I sorta want to go, I also told her I didn't know how to dance, but she said that was okay too, I could come over to her house, her mother would teach me.

The desire to crumple the thing up and throw it in the trash almost overwhelmed her, but she didn't. That Jody girl's manipulation obviously didn't work in the long haul. Tears, no less.

And inviting him over to her house so she and her mom could teach him how to dance. Really. Yeah right, the girl's mother wouldn't be anywhere in sight.

She gritted her teeth and read on. He wasted a whole page writing about cows, calves and his monster feed bill, then there must have been a break in time, or either his pen ran out of ink, and he got a different-colored one.

Okay, I did my due, I took her, her father even let us take his Cadillac nice ride, but dancing isn't for me, the music was too loud and weird, and all that jumping up and down flinging your arms around, the band only played a couple of slow numbers, those weren't too bad, but well Jody is going off to College next year and well she wanted me to promise I'd go too, kind of hinted that her daddy would loan me the money, but one more year and I'm done with school, figure with another fifty or sixty head I can live off my calf crop, especially if I can lease some good pasture land.

Been doing ranch day work on Saturdays, one of these days I might make a cowboy, and well I didn't tell Jody this, but I'm not for sale, I don't care how much money her daddy has.

She laughed out loud. "Good for you, Samuel." She realized she was talking to herself, but hey, he had a level head on him even back then. "Okay, Lord, forgive me for hating on that Jody girl, and thank You for keeping Samuel single all these years."

Wouldn't it be cool if he'd saved himself, too? Could be. His letters sounded like once he got saved....

Her nose dripped, and she grabbed another tissue and blew it. That was really too much to even hope for. She gulped more watered-down tea, it was still pretty sweet though, then read on.

Family news, boring, but it would be nice having it to refer to once she met all of his relatives, then another ink color change.

Mom and dad came yesterday, broke my heart, they're driving this old junker car, and well both of them are in pretty bad shape, PawPaw offered to let them stay, but only if they'd agreed to house arrest. I thought they were going to agree for a while, but then

*turned out all they wanted was money, we didn't give them any,
PawPaw did put some gas in their car, and we prayed for them like
we always do, I told them Jesus could heal them, but neither
seemed interested.*

*Mary Esther don't ever even try that stuff not even one time,
PawPaw sat me down after they drove off and we had like the
millionth drug talk, and for sure I will learn from their mistakes.
Please you too, I couldn't stand it if you got involved with drugs.*

I love you, please come home, I miss you so much.
Samuel Baylor

She pulled the missive to her heart and thought of her own
junior year. Wasn't thinking about him much at all then. With all
her extra-curricular activities and singing at churches, too, she'd
been too busy.

That was right about the time she'd started composing, too.
Wow, that's when she'd written her first country song.

She leaned back and savored that first royalty check again.
One hundred and forty-two dollars, nothing like some of the really
fat ones that came later, but that's when she knew....

Her nasty-mouthed phone rooster crowed his little red head
off. She pried one eye open. The sun shone bright through the lace
curtains on the east window. She touched her cell. Oh, gracious,
she had better get it in gear.

And she hadn't even decided what to sing either, much less
practiced.

Oh, Lord, what am I going to wear? Or sing?

DO YOU TRUST ME?

Of course, I do. You know I do.

But He didn't tell her what to sing.

Chapter Twelve ✟♥♫♪

Sunday morning in Cuthand Methodist's new
sanctuary, the last note of the last hymn drifted off. The song
leader smiled at Samuel. He nodded, filled his lungs, stood, then
strolled to the pulpit. "Good Morning."

A few audible greetings sounded, but most folks only nodded
or smiled. He closed his eyes and waited. A peace settled over him,
and a scripture came to his heart.

"To find a Godly wife is to find a good thing." He smiled,
scanning the congregation and the reactions the statement brought.
The Lord cracked him up sometimes with His excellent sense of
humor.

Was Samuel preaching to the people or himself? Guess he'd
have to see exactly where the Holy Spirit was going with that train
of thought.

For the next few minutes, he spoke directly to the young
ladies, quoting the scriptures that came to him on the subject of
being good wives then after using some of the mothers in the Word
as examples.

Then he switched to address the young men and boys. "Now,
guys." He paused and searched the two dozen or so males of
marrying age or soon to be. "The onus is more on you than the
ladies."

No amens sounded, but their eyes remained fixed on him. A
few even sat forward and leaned on the pew in front of them. It
didn't seem any tuned him out either. Maybe, like him, they were
waiting to see what God's message would say to them.

The topic definitely proved to be one they all were obviously
interested in.

"God is faithful. He will not allow the devil to tempt you more
than you can bear. That's found in the first book of Corinthians,

chapter ten, verse thirteen." He loved it when a particular scripture's location came to him.

A blessing the Lord granted him at times, usually only when he stood in front of a congregation. He knew the word well on his own, but rarely remembered most of their addresses.

"Doctor Luke reported Jesus said to pray that you don't enter into temptation. I'd advise that you not even put yourself in the position to be tempted."

He grinned at the serious expressions facing him and at himself for agreeing, even volunteering; to be Mary Esther's carpenter. So... he wasn't only talking to those sitting in the pews.

"Once upon a time, a young lady talked me into taking her to a dance. It was the first and last time I went to such, but the shindig wasn't the problem. Most of ya'll know my grandfather reared me, and PawPaw had a rule.

"He called it Cinderella Liberty. I had to be home before midnight, period. Well, the young lady's father loaned me the use of his car, claiming his daughter couldn't go to the prom in an old diesel truck.

"Anyway, my date wanted to go to this big after-prom bash at North Lake. She assured me her parents were not expecting her home until very late if at all. She said we could party all night, that she'd even packed an overnight bag and had it in the trunk."

He paused and searched out the parents' reactions. "After a brief discussion—it did get rather heated—I took her home, early. Praise God for old men with absolute rules and firm hands for the young men in their charge.

"Parents, you'll answer for how you train up your children. Fathers, the bulk of that responsibility belongs to you." That drew a few amens, most from the women, and more nods of agreement. A wife or two elbowed her husband.

"That night... the party turned into a drunken brawl and many of the young men ended up incarcerated the next morning. The young lady apologized profusely the next time I saw her at school and thanked me for escorting her home."

The congregation's attention seemed intense.

"Not too long ago, maybe only a hundred years, a young lady was not allowed to be alone with a young man. At a marriageable age, if interested, he went courting, and the young couple would always be chaperoned to maintain the woman's honor and reputation.

"Our nation's morals are in decline, but just because the wicked maintain a thing is okay, God doesn't change. Sin is still sin.

"That prom party changed several lives." A few older heads nodded; of course they remembered. Who didn't? "A bit before dawn, one of my classmates shot and killed his ex-best-friend.

"The young lady they fought over gave birth to her dead lover's baby eight months later." He glanced at the clock. Almost noon, he best wrap things up. "Now my PawPaw told me that it's a wise man who can learn from another's mistakes, but a fool that doesn't even learn from his own.

"Be wise, guys. You don't have to sow any wild oats. Why reap dour consequences of society's acceptable behavior? Treat the ladies as if they were your mother or sister, or better, your grandmother.

"Show them respect, protect their honor." He held his hands out. "God bless you, and keep you, and Lord, bless our meal and the hands that prepared it. Amen."

A chorus of amens followed and the piano player softly keyed a departing song, then like most dinner-on-the-grounds Sundays he'd attended, the women hurried to set everything out and the boys scrambled to be first in the chow line.

Only a few hung around and shook his hand. A couple of ladies had heard about him and Mary Esther singing at Big Woods and were thrilled when he told them she was on her way.

✝ ♥ ♫♪ •*•♪♫ ✝

Mary Esther glanced at her phone, slowed, turned south like it wanted, then pretty quick, made a right going back west. Good, only one more turn. She leaned back and set her cruise control on fifty in the fifty-five miles per hour zone.

Getting there a few minutes sooner wasn't worth speeding, except she could hardly wait to tell him about the Church of Christ service.

Mercy, she'd never ever... Oh, if only he would have been there. Okay, new rule, no more going anywhere or agreeing to do anything without him. Period. End of discussion.

The parking lot testified to a decent crowd. She pulled in and hurried to the entrance marked fellowship hall then swung the door open. Most of the Methodists already filled tables, with plates overflowing. She didn't spot Samuel.

The serving line had thinned to four deep, but at least they weren't all through. Not too bad considering DeKalb being thirty-six miles from Cuthand, but here in God's country three cars at an intersection was a jam.

With no traffic, it didn't take long to get anywhere, and forget red lights. Hardly ever had one of those to hold anyone up.

There he was. Just as she spotted him, Samuel looked up and grinned. He extracted himself from a small group of boys and young men then hurried to her side. "Hey, Baby, how'd it go?"

"So awesome I could hardly believe it. Chucky's mother wanted me to sing "Amazing Grace." That went okay. Then oh mercy, Samuel, the Lord gave me a new song, and I sang it right out.

The congregation caught it, and they joined in singing it with me, and...." She chuckled and leaned in. "They clapped at the end. It was so sweet! Have you ever heard such a thing?"

He shrugged. "I've only been to a few Church of Christ services; knew they didn't use instruments, but no clapping either?"

"Nope, not that I've ever known. But they sure did this morning, and it was awesome."

"Sure would have loved being there, but it was great here, too."

"What'd you preach on?"

He smiled. "Finding a good wife."

"Really? Do they have a tape ministry so I could get a copy?"

"I don't think so."

A man about Samuel's age holding a three-and-a-half or four-year-old girl slipped in next to her. He looked real familiar, but....

"Hey, Mary Esther Robbins. Remember me?"

"Well, kind of sort of, yes and no. You definitely look a bit... It's in the eyes. Happen to have a picture of you when you were twelve?"

The man laughed. "Not on me. I'm Dusty Singleton; I was a grade ahead of you guys."

"Oh, Dusty! Sure. Wow, you got tall. Is this your daughter?"

"It is. Mallory, say hello to Miss Mary Esther."

The little angel buried her head beneath her daddy's chin against his chest. "Hello, Miss Mary Esther."

"Hello, Mallory, you're a very pretty little girl."

"What do you say, puddin'? Can you thank Miss Mary?"

She put her finger in her mouth and wiggled in his arms. "Thank you."

He faced Samuel. "I was at that party, and it was so much worse than you made it out."

"Praise the Lord that PawPaw kept a tight rein on me."

"Took me most of the summer to work off what that little bash cost me between all the fines and court costs. Only time I've ever spent a night in jail."

"At least you survived."

"Amen." He looked to her. "Good to see you again, Mary Esther. Hope you guys come back. We were headed for some sugar." The man nuzzled his baby girl then headed to the dessert table.

"You hungry?"

"Yes, I am. Skipped breakfast. Have you already eaten?"

"No, ma'am. Been waiting for you."

Once there, he handed her a Styrofoam plate plastic silverware and a napkin as though she couldn't get it herself. But it was cute him waiting on her. He put his hand on her back and eased her forward.

His touch weakened her knees. Oh, why couldn't he wrap her up and never let her go? Could it ever be?

Every kind of delicious casserole and meat, vegetables and salads filled the food table. Angel eggs, bread, and rolls filled any blank spaces.

She grinned remembering what Grami used to call the fancy eggs—her daddy's mother had been her favorite—then loaded her plate with one tablespoon each of half of the scrumptious-looking dishes.

The dinners on the grounds could prove dangerous to a girl's waistline. Couldn't indulge in them very often or her new wardrobe wouldn't fit. Her skirts would be more forgiving than jeans though.

She found two empty seats together, sat, and waited on him. Wasn't long until he joined her. "It's already been blessed, dig in."

Took three bites before it hit her. "What party was Dusty talking about?"

"The one after the prom."

"Your junior year?"

"Yes, how'd you know?"

"Duh, you told me in one of my letters."

"Oh, yeah, I wrote that down didn't I?"

"Yes, well I don't remember seeing anything about an after-the-prom bash. So you took Jody to it?"

"No, as a matter of fact, I didn't. She wanted to go, but it was getting late, and midnight was my curfew."

"Yay, PawPaw. So why was it so bad? What happened?"

"The least of it was that six guys and two girls got drunk and ended up in jail. Two others, best buds once, also had too much to drink and ended up in a big fight over a girl. It turned deadly."

"Oh no."

"It gets worse. The girl they were fighting over delivered the dead guy's baby eight months later."

"Oh mercy...." In a flash, another life flickered across her soul's stage. In that alternate reality, she and Samuel suffered all the pains and struggles of growing up together. "Could that be why Daddy had to leave?"

"That what?"

"My Daddy. If he hadn't gone to live in Heaven, I wonder how different our lives would have been. And his and mother's, too. Think we would have...?"

Samuel set his fork down and took her hand in both of his. "That's one of those questions we'll have to save for when we see Him face to face."

She agreed, then after almost cleaning her plate—one celery casserole had curry, and she couldn't do curry—she figured now was as good a time as any. "So what happened between you and Jody?"

He shrugged. "Nothing."

"Like totally nothing?" Mary Esther had no right in the least to be jealous, but if there had been something there, didn't she need to know?

He smiled then leaned in close. "Let me rephrase, counselor, I never kissed her or hugged her or did anything other than holding her way out at arms' length the three times I slow danced with her. Is that nothing enough?"

"Yes. I guess so." Her cheeks warmed. She hated to blush. "I was just asking, okay?"

He snickered, but didn't answer her.

"So what happened to good ol' Jody?"

"Don't know; her family moved back to Oklahoma if memory serves. I never saw her again after school was out that year."

"I never could place her so I looked her up on Facebook."

"They didn't move to Clarksville until you were long gone. So did you find her?"

"There were about two hundred Jody Reynolds, none from Clarksville, and since I didn't know what she looked like…?"

He smiled. "I've heard of that Facebook. What's it for?"

"It's all about reaching out, connecting with old friends, meeting new ones."

Two preteen girls appeared across the table from her. The oldest-looking one smiled. "You're Mary Esther, right? The Mary Esther?"

"Yes, I guess I am." She smiled.

Both girls produced a fresh napkin and extended them toward her. "Can we have your autograph, please?" They looked at each other with puckered faces. "Are you staying for tonight's service? Oh, please say yes. You could sing a solo. I know they'd let you."

Samuel patted the closest one's forearm. "She is staying, and we'll see. The Lord may want something different."

"What could be better than Mary Esther singing a solo?"

"How about a trio? You girls sing?"

Both giggled then shook their heads in unison. "Not up in front of everyone."

✞ ♥ ♫♪ •*•♪ ♫ ✞

Samuel loved the way she handled the little ladies, almost as much as he loved that she was jealous of him, especially over a girl he hadn't seen in fifteen years. But oh Lord. Then it hit him.

What if instead of some scoundrel catching her fancy, the cad had slipped her something? He'd heard about date rape drugs. If she hadn't been responsible....

Could that be it?

Oh, Lord, should it still count if someone forced her?

✝♥♫♪ *Chapter Thirteen*

Samuel tried to focus on the guessing game Mary
Esther had roped him into, but couldn't. Regarding her status, no
scripture came to mind, and so far, the Lord hadn't put anything on
his heart that would guide him.

But that was it.

Someone had forced her.

Had to be, right?

She elbowed him then whispered. "You are not helping."

"Sorry." He put her condition out of his mind and
concentrated on the game. Being her partner would be enough. The
Apostle Paul didn't have a wife or children, but God still blessed
him with so many sons in the Lord.

Thank you, Father, for bringing her back to me.

The other couple hollered something and then both clapped.

She elbowed him again. "You are not paying attention. What's
wrong with you? We lost." She stood and extended her hand.
"Come on, loser, let's find a game we can win."

He let her pull him up then once out of earshot of the group
still playing, he leaned in. "Mercy, girl, lighten up. You have not
changed one iota. Well…" He shut his mouth. Best stop going
there.

"Well what?"

He exhaled. Know the truth, and the truth would set you free.
"Well, maybe an iota or two."

"How's that?"

"Well, before you were pretty, past cute by at least a mile, and
now, well, your physical looks are only surpassed by your inner

beauty." He smiled. "Even if you do go around calling people names."

✞♥♫♪ •*•♪♫✞

"I'm sorry. You're not a loser, and thank you, kind sir." Mary Esther squeezed his hand, the one that should be wrapped around her. "So what are we doing this evening?"

"Don't know exactly, but they want us to start at five instead of the usual six."

"Why's that?"

"Chores, I guess. Most everyone hasn't gone home, so…" He glanced up. She followed his gaze to the big clock on the far wall; four-fifteen. "In a few minutes, if they do it like last time, we'll put the tables away and get all the chairs back up."

She tugged on his hand. "Come on then, they're pitching washers outside. I know we can win at that."

Apparently the tossing skill she had acquired as a child had rusted somewhat, didn't even get out of the first round. She hated losing, but spending time with Samuel, she was a winner in every way.

Only needed to find a way for him to ask her to marry him, then all would be right in her world. But he seemed so distracted. Maybe he was trying to figure out the best way to propose. On one knee or taking her out.

Should she ask him about Ralph? Tell him it wasn't fair to count him as her parent. Gracious, her daddy raised her for twelve years, and Samuel knew what kind of man he was. Even still said mercy all the time like her daddy.

A grin started in her heart and made its way to her lips.

What a great, Christ-like man he'd been, a perfect example of the fruits of the Holy Spirit in operation: love, gentleness, patience, kindness, faithfulness, joy, peace, goodness, and self control.

Galatians five twenty-two, an easy scripture address to remember since it was her birthday. She loved having that for her birthday scripture. Oooo, she needed a song for it.

Lord?

What if he's waiting on a ring? He could have ordered one online. She scoffed a guttural sound at her own self. He didn't even have a cell phone, much less internet service. What was the hold up?

Certainly did love his remark that she was beautiful inside and out, and she loved him with her whole heart.

Without a doubt, and she'd only been back…had it only a week? Yet she knew that she knew. And besides, the Lord said.…

Ralph and her mother—they had to be the reason for his reluctance. But mercy, forget her daddy, she'd been around PawPaw more than she'd been around her heathen stepdad.

And what about Mimi Lady? Now there was a Godly woman. That's what she needed to do, call her Mimi and have her pray Samuel to his senses.

"Last call." A young man stood at the church's side entrance. "Last call everyone, you've got five minutes."

Mary Esther looked from the young man to Samuel. "What's that all about?"

"Last shot at leftovers, the ladies are getting ready to clean up."

"Oh, I better go help." She smiled at him then hurried inside.

The church mothers protested. She was company, but in the end, they let her do a little. It was only right for her to do her part.

Her mother and Mimi Lady would switch her good if they ever found out she was freeloading and letting all the older women handle the work. Well, maybe more like subjecting her to a good talking to, but that was bad enough.

Then it was time for church, but instead of the regular configuration, the chairs had been put in three circles. Okay, that was different. She found Samuel's Bible and sat down next to it.

Calling the services to order, he opened with a prayer. She not only loved the sound of his voice, but the sweet casual way he spoke to the Lord. Like a child talking to his father. No formal rote trying to sound all holier than thou.

Just natural communication between loved ones.

He took his seat, then an older man—one of the washer-pitching pros—got up and belted out three hymns. She loved that they had so many instruments, not at all like any Methodist church she'd ever been in.

She knew "I'll Fly Away" and sang along, harmonizing, but the other two were new to her, probably Methodist favorites, and she'd grown up Southern Baptist.

When he nodded at Samuel, he stood and walked to the circles' center. "Blessings, folks! I am so humbled that so many of you chose to stay, but..." He smiled at her. "Well, I'm wondering if my best friend here had something to do with that."

He bowed his head.

Her cheeks warmed, but she'd like it so much better if he introduced her as his fiancée, or better still, his wife.

Oh Lord, You said You made me for him. That was You, I know it, so how long do I have to wait? He's so the desire of my heart, I've never been surer about anything in my life. I've wasted all those years feeding my stupid pride over thinking he didn't write. That kept me from realizing Your Truth.

"Amen."

Her heart stopped clean smooth. She looked at him. Had she been praying out loud? She checked her ears and exhaled. No, praise God. He was saying amen to his own prayer, right?

"The wicked hate rules, but love to rule."

Amens aplenty came from every direction.

"Grace, now there's an interesting concept. God's amazing grace. But what exactly does that mean?" He quoted several scriptures verbatim. How much time had he spent memorizing the Word?

She'd heard and read all the verses he cited, quoted many of them herself, but she'd definitely need her concordance and probably an hour or two getting prepared with all their addresses, but he hadn't spent any time that afternoon, she knew that for sure.

Remembering him saying he never planned what to say and about fresh manna, she sat in amazement that the Lord just gave the message to him. Wow, it wasn't only His grace that was amazing.

Hey, that sounded like a song.

The first lines came into her head on a beautiful melody.

'It isn't only Your grace that's amazing, the sound is as sweet of Your faithfulness too. You never slumber or sleep, You've promised my soul to keep, and when I get in too deep, Your love always lifts me.'

Oh wow, she loved her new song, how it incorporated other old familiar hymns.

"Now during the Dark Ages."

Dark Ages, was that when the dinosaurs roamed? Why was he going there?

"The Church had fallen into apostasy, even to the point that popes and priests were selling indulgences."

Oh, okay, not that far back.

"What's that, Samuel? Indulgences?" She turned toward the voice, a guy in the back.

"If you can believe it," Samuel shook his head, "free sins. They did exclude murder and such, but in their system of confession and penance, buying an indulgence made perfect sense. Some of those priests could be brutal on what they made their parishioners do to achieve forgiveness."

He looked around, turning in a slow circle. "Folks, the same lie is still being perpetuated today. Now, I've never been to a Catholic mass, but I have seen a few on TV where someone goes into the confessional.

"The priest opens the little window and hears what that person did, then tells them how many Our Fathers or Hail Marys they have to say to be forgiven."

Heads nodded and he continued.

"It doesn't work that way. God requires perfection, and we can be perfect. All our sins were washed away at the cross."

"At the Cross" started playing in her head. 'Alas, and did my Savior bleed.' Oh not now. She didn't want to lose her new song. Should she get up and go sing what He'd given her into her phone so she wouldn't forget?

Forcing "At the Cross" away, she silently went over "It Isn't Only Your Grace" in her head again.

Whew, she still had it.

"And best of all, it's free. We don't have to do anything other than accept His gift. Then He goes about making us into the image of His Perfect Son."

He waited for the congregation to react, and they did. Seemed they loved him as much as she did. What about pastoring a congregation? He could definitely pull them in, and she could help.

That would be awesome, but would it fall into his category of not merchandising the Gospel?

"There's a mentality in some churches today, that if you backslide and then come to your senses, that you have to work your way back into God's good graces. That's wrong.

"The Word says if we confess our sins, He's faithful and just to forgive and He doesn't remember them anymore.

"I know that's hard to wrap your understanding around, but if the Blood washes them away, who am I to remember them? Jesus made the ultimate sacrifice, freely gave His life for ours—me, you, and anyone who will accept it.

"No longer do we have to spill the blood of bulls and goats to roll our sins over for another year. No. On the cross, Jesus said, 'It is finished.' and gave up the ghost then went to hell in my place."

He wiped at his cheeks, sniffed once, then blinked back tears.

A fire sparked, rose in Mary Esther's belly, then erupted. She stood and sang the new song she heard. "The Blood of Christ declares I am healed, by His precious blood, Love is revealed. His rich red blood, it cleanses me. The blood of Yeshua bought my liberty."

Turning a slow full circle as she walked down the center aisle, she met the eyes of the folks. "It's not the blood of goats or ram, it's the Blood of the Great I Am, it's not the blood of a mere man. Praise God for the Blood that ca-a-a-n, Wash away my sins and make me white as snow, give me power to walk in the way I need to go. It gives me strength to stand from day to day. His redeeming blood points me to The Way!

"Oh, the Blood, the Blood, God's precious Blood, it's full of power for this very hour! The Blood, the Blood, our covenant. The life is in the Blood."

Wow, He gave her two more verses. The second showed her The Truth, and the third The Life. The Way, Truth, and Life. She loved it.

She sank to her knees and worshipped, thanking God for such a new song, extolled His majesty and basked in His presence, oblivious to anything but Him Who sat on the throne.

Weeping pulled her back to the now.

Two teenage boys and an older girl, maybe in her twenties stood in front of Samuel.

He had his arm over the shoulder of one of the boys with his head close to the young man's ear. The sobs came from behind her. She glanced around. Two older ladies cried openly, but both were shedding tears of joy, so obviously intent on the young people with Samuel.

Praise God! He had used her and Samuel to bring these three to Jesus. Oh, if only it could be that way for the rest of her life. That's what she longed for, bringing souls into the Kingdom while praising God.

Rising, she went to pray with the young woman. What a great honor to help her, pray with her, to become one of God's children. Was there anything better?

The evening flew by. Samuel stayed and prayed or counseled with any and all. But by twos and threes, the folks drifted off. Finally, it was just him and her standing next to her sedan illuminated by the church's security lights.

"What about having our own church?"

"No, I've been offered several, but the Lord has something different in mind for me."

Oh no, was this why he hadn't asked her? But God had told her…. "Care to share?"

He touched the tip of her nose. "I'd love to, but I need to get home and feed. We can talk about it on the way to…" His eyes widened slightly and his forehead wrinkled inquisitively. "Where is the sound studio?"

"Paris."

"Okay, that'll give us time to talk."

She wanted him to stay and tell her his heart, but understood he had chores. "What time in the morning?"

"I'll be there early. I'd like to get the house down on her blocks before anything happens."

"Like what could happen?"

"A storm, lots of things. The wooden blocks are temporary; I'll like it better when your home's sitting on concrete."

"Okay, I'll see you then. Want donuts or sausage biscuits?"

Oh, how she did love that grin of his.

"Surprise me."

She pulled out first then hit the brake and slid her phone to life. He stopped next to her and got out. "Something wrong?"

"No, I just wasn't sure which way to go."

He pointed north. "Take this road straight into Clarksville, nothing to it."

She did as he said, but still checked her phone. He was right, and in no time, she entered her rented room. Sure would be glad when she could move into the house. With plenty still to do, it'd be a while yet.

Still, getting it in place—and on concrete—excited her and set her decorating juices to flowing.

She'd pinned about a thousand great ideas she could incorporate. But she'd have to go back through them, and that took time. And so did everything, the house, church, reading his letters.

All good things, blessings. She glanced at the stack of unread missives, but instead of reading more, she knelt by her bed.

"Father God, bless you and thank you. Thank you for leading me back to Clarksville, for giving me two new awesome songs tonight, for helping the guys get my house moved, for keeping Samuel single and bringing him into my life again, for creating me for him.

"I have so much to be grateful for. Your blessings overwhelm and humble me.

"Please, Lord, get it through his thick skull that he needs me, and reveal to him that I need him just as much. Here I am, all alone in this room, and he's out there in English, in that little trailer all by himself.

"Show him, Lord. Tell him now, please, Father, even as I pray. You've made us for each other, so tell him. He knows Your voice. Speak to Him like you did me.

"Mercy, Lord, isn't twenty years without him long enough?"

She chuckled.

"And could You make it happen tomorrow? I really need to be about planning my wedding."

Chapter Fourteen ✝♥♫♪

Samuel had already started lowering her house in the hour and a half before she got there with donuts and coffee. "Morning, boss." He stood and dusted himself off.

She handed him a steaming paper cup then extended the goodie box. He took a glazed. "Sure did like your blood song. Want to do that one today, too."

"Yes, God confirms it. I was thinking the same thing, and He gave me another one while you were preaching."

"Okay, want to do that one, too? How many can we do?"

She smiled. "Time is money, and we'll be on your dime, so you tell me. With no practice…" She shrugged. "How can I say how long one might take?"

How much was a soul worth? He could not name the price.

"Guess we go until I run out of cash then, or you run out of songs."

"How long you been here? Have you lowered it any?"

Raising an arm into the sky, the one with the last bite of that first donut, he laughed. "Three whole inches at least. Are you blind, woman?"

Her eyebrows arched. He loved that look, her teasing expression. She was twelve years old again, and his heart filled afresh with an innocent and pure love for her.

"Three whole inches, huh?" She stood back stroking her chin, carefully examining the structure. "Ah, yes, I see it now for certain. My home is definitely closer to the ground." She grinned. "You know, might even be four."

He glanced at the house. "Whatever, you need to call Highlands, have them deliver us thirty-three solid concrete blocks. All my bud had was the ones with holes, and we don't want those."

"Sure, anything else?"

Yes, he wanted a thousand kisses and for her to grab hold of his hand and never let go. But he didn't tell her that, couldn't, not until the Lord told him if her condition was acceptable or not. "No, that'll do us for today."

He worked her hard all the way to dinnertime, not so much on purpose, but she didn't want to hire any labor. "We best stop there."

She frowned. "Why? We're so close."

Man, frowning, smiling, working, teasing, competing, praising, focusing, embarrassed or loving. He loved her every expression, just being around her. Lord, if that's all I can have, all I ever get, just looking on her face, then so be it. But please, have mercy on me. "I'm cashing my rain check."

"What did you say?"

"Remember? Rio Verde. You offered, and I took a rain check, so now, I'm cashing it in. We've got time to eat and still get to Paris by one if we leave now."

She pulled her phone out and frowned at the thing. "Wow, where did the morning go?" She tucked it back into her skirt pocket. "Okay, you're right, it's getting late."

✝ ♥ ♫♪ •*•♪ ♫ ✝

He wasn't quite the pepper belly Mary Esther was, but he had scooped half his little cup of hot sauce while he devoured chips two to her one.

She loved watching him eat, totally enjoyed the way he did things, all slow and deliberate as though he'd pondered and reached a learned decision. She loved his laugh, the sound of his voice, even his thick skull.

Stubbornness, in certain instances, could be a really good thing.

But mercy, him not seeing that the Lord had make her for him and that she needed some time to plan out the wedding… seemed that took thick-skulled to a whole new level.

"What are you frowning about?"

She put on her happy face. "Me? Frowning? Is that what I was doing just now?"

"Yes, you sure were, so why? Care to share?"

"Not now, but I do want to hear about what the Lord has in store. That is, if you know yet?"

"Sure, you ready?"

"Yes, sir." She reached for the bill, but he snatched it up.

"My idea, I'll get this one."

"What about the rain check?"

"I've still got it."

So gallant, her love. Once she cleared town, she prompted him one more time.

"First of all, I've never shared this with anyone."

"Okay, fine. You know I can keep a secret. What is it?"

"I don't want to sound like I'm something I'm not."

She glanced over. He looked dead serious. "Ha! So what are you not? Am I going to have to come all the way through the back door here, Baylor? Come on. What?"

"The Lord wants me to start a school."

"Really? Wow. Like a Christian school? All twelve grades or just elementary to start with and work up from there?" No wonder he didn't want to tell anyone.

"Christian, yes, but not for kids."

"Okay. Guess I'm not getting the picture. Exactly what kind of school?"

"One for prophets."

"Okay, like Elijah and Isaiah, and Daniel you mean? Those guys?"

"Kind of, more like Samuel. He's the one who started the original school of the prophets."

"Double wow. That's cool. So when? Where? Can I help?"

"Don't know, downtown Clarksville, and yes, I hope so."

She replayed the questions so he knew where but not when and... "So how can I help?"

"You could start a choir."

"What? Singing prophets?" But glory bumps trumped any mirth. They spread from her heart and engulfed her, setting her skin on edge. She wanted to pull over and dance on the side of the road. How awesome. She'd prayed about prophetic songs. Asked the Lord for them.

And now she was going to the school of the prophets to start a choir. "Yes. That would be great. I'd love having a choir, but if we're not starting a church, where would we sing?"

"Wherever the Lord leads. Besides, in case you've never noticed, there's not a lot of lost folks in church anyway."

"Oh wow, triple wow. You're talking like out on the street, aren't you? Oh, Lord, so much more than I ever thought or imagined. Wouldn't that be something? I mean, it'd be just like Jesus." A second wave of joy crashed over her like a tsunami. Great, stupendous, absolutely fantastic. It was going to be great. "Sorry, I need some time here."

Checking her rear-view mirror, she whipped her car off onto the shoulder and jumped out. Keeping on the grassy shoulder, she clapped and twirled, pivoted several three-sixties and whooped.

Slipping back behind the wheel, she faced him. "Sorry, I couldn't help it. This is awesome. Like King David bringing the ark home to Jerusalem."

The remodeling would just have to wait. Her savings would go a long way toward funding the school. She could live in his trailer. It'd be fine, more than fine. The little fifth-wheel would be plenty big enough for two—or three.

She glanced at him. "You do you want children, right?"

"Yes, ma'am, I love babies."

"Okay, you said downtown Clarksville. Have you got a specific place in mind?"

"The old furniture store, Slaton's. The one the tornado hit."

"The one with the metal facade roof?"

"One and the same."

"Okay, I'm in, lock, stock, and barrel whatever that means. All the way. I'm with you. Let's do it, like tomorrow. Forget my house. That can wait."

He laughed. "No, we're going to finish your home, and we will do the school and choir in God's time. Remember what the Word says about those that wait upon the Lord?"

"Yes, of course I do. Anyone ever tell you that you're no fun? It's downright mean to get me all exited and then tell me to wait."

"I want to be David, not Saul."

"Yes. So do I, but…" Waaaah. She hated waiting. But…

Oh Lord, is that what You're doing? Teaching me patience?

With only one wrong turn and fifteen minutes to spare, she and Google located the studio, smaller than most she'd been in, but the equipment looked top notch.

She couldn't believe how smooth "Up From the Grave" went, and what Samuel said was even better than at Big Woods, and her part went great, too, especially taking into account she hadn't warmed up properly.

Of course she would have liked another take or six, but mercy, that was just the perfectionist in her.

Then on to her "The Blood of Christ" song. He threw her a curve and wanted her to do that as a solo. So fast and peppy, and with so many words to every bar, she messed up the second verse twice, but then got it right and belted it out all the way through.

"How was that?"

"Excellent. That second verse sounds a little tricky. But you nailed it."

"Want another take? And how about you coming in on the chorus? I heard a harmony, but it's hard to harmonize with yourself."

"Not yet, go ahead and do the new one, then we'll see how much money I've got left."

"Want to help?"

He extended his hand. "If something comes to me I'll give you a squeeze."

It didn't, and she sang that one all the way through, this no-practice thing worked pretty awesome. Although it could be him holding her hand had something to do with it. "That went well, what now?"

He let go of her hand and held up one finger. "Be right back."

She closed her eyes.

Oh Lord, thank You for putting it in Samuel's heart to do these songs and—mercy—give them away. That is so like You, and thank You for bringing me home and for the school and choir.

What pearls of great price! She opened her eyes. That's what she needed to do, sell her land, or part of it anyway, and buy that building, and yes, Lord. It all belongs to You anyway.

The door opened. "We've time for one more."

"Okay great, want to do the Blood song again?"

"No, let's sing one together, about the end of the age." He extended his hand, and she grabbed it. He filled his lungs. "Days of trouble."

She came in without skipping a beat. "Days of dread."

"Days of tribulation are just ahead."

Wow, he rhymed it. Without knowing exactly what came next, she didn't even hesitate, just opened her mouth. "Horrible days such as the world has never known." A sweet essence wafted in the air. She smelled His presence and breathed Him in deep.

"The sun is getting hotter every day."

"The earth groans with labor in so many ways."

"Stars will be falling from the sky."

"There'll be nowhere to hide."

He squeezed her hand and mouthed together in the short rest. "But keep your eyes on the Eastern skies. Lift up your head, your redemption draweth ni-i-i-i-igh." The notes stair-stepped up. What fun!

"God's beloved Son, the Pure and Holy One, He's coming soon! And His reward is in His hand."

Wow, what a totally awesome chorus. She loved it, and the Lord was giving the new song to Samuel at the same time as her. Amazing, so amazing. He'd started the second verse.

He swept a hand high as if showing off the ceiling. "The heavens will open, behold a white horse."

She could see it! "Its rider is Faithful and True, of course!"

"On His head there is written a name no one knows but He Himself."

"His eyes are bright as flames of fire."

"And on His head there will be many crowns."

"From His mouth comes a sword, an iron scepter He carries in His hand."

Then they were to the chorus again and sang it together. The song went on for one more verse through Armageddon and the millennial reign. She repeated the last line slower. "He's coming soon, and His reward is in His hand."

Samuel did the same, then God gave her new words for the chorus' tune, but the man didn't sing them with her.

"He's the King of Kings and Lord of Lords. All knees will bow and proclaim that He is Lord. I'm His beloved one. My Bridegroom is God's Son, and I'll be one with Him throughout all eternity!"

Samuel ended it. "Days of trouble, days of dread."

The last note drifted off.

She wiped her cheeks. "I love you, Samuel Levi Baylor."

✝♥♫♪ Chapter Fifteen

The afterglow faded with each click of the odometer. In its place, the reality of him not saying I love you back seeped into Mary Esther's heart of hearts, dulled her hope and caused her to doubt she'd heard from God at all.

It must have been her own self, thinking it so loud in her head because she so wanted it to be.

But now that she'd returned and spent so much time around him, she realized she loved him and never wanted anyone like she wanted him. Couldn't first dibs work? She kept glancing over.

What was he thinking? He seemed lost in his own thoughts. Was he trying to figure out how to tell her he loved her like what? A sister?

He'd told her in his letter that he loved her, would always love her, but he wrote it twenty years ago, a lifetime. She didn't think he was in love with someone else, but probably should have read the rest of his letters.

Maybe she could have found out something she needed to know. Was she fooling herself with thinking he was the one she'd been saving herself for?

"I need tomorrow off."

She looked over then back to the road. "Okay, sure. What's up?"

"The auction."

"Why? What are you selling?"

"My herd. I'm going to sell out."

"But… I thought you loved ranching."

"It's time. To start the school."

"God said that? That it's time? Can you use any help?"

"All I can get. If you're volunteering, yes. I'd like that."

A chill washed over her then in a day vision of some sort, his cows grazed her bottoms. "Hey, instead of taking the little darlings to auction, how about selling them to me?"

"Thought you were short of cash."

"I've still got over twenty thousand in the bank. I figured it'd take that and some more to get the house done right, but I own the land free and clear. Even at twenty cents on the dollar, I can borrow more than enough to buy your cows, and if I remember right, the banks in these parts loan money on beeves."

"They do, but that's a risky business. Prices drop, grain and hay go up. The bank wants their money, no matter what."

"But didn't you say the calf crop paid the expenses plus enough for you to live off of? How much does fence cost?"

"We could hot wire it for not a lot. I have some of what you'd need. Have to build you a corral, and…"

"And what?"

"Oh, I'm getting ahead of myself; we best pray about this, I'd hate myself forever if you lost your dad's place."

"Sure, we can do that, but just now, I saw your cows grazing my bottoms, and we can get enough money to buy whatever equipment we'll need, and the Lord will bless it, just like He's going to bless those songs."

Raising his brows, he glanced at the ground then back at her, but said nothing.

"Mercy, Samuel, how many folks are going to get saved listening to our songs, except they're not ours. I mean He gave them to us, but then told you to give them away, so…"

He held his hands up. "Whoa now, slow down, girl. You're going ninety miles an hour. Let's take it easy. The Word says line upon line, precept on precept, here a little, there a little."

She looked down at her odometer; she was only doing seventy-five, but he was right. She needed to take it easy, go slower, get it right. That was probably one of her worst traits, always being in a hurry.

So many times with the band, she'd gotten ahead of God. Not that He didn't reel her back in and forgive her and used what she'd done for her good in the end.

"Okay, you're right. But we can at least go ahead and stop by the bank and pick up a loan application, couldn't we? And then we'll… Where's a good place to buy some hay equipment?"

"You've already sold us your hay, remember?"

"Oh, yeah, that's right. Your neighbor's in partners with us on the hay. So does he have all the machinery we need?"

"What he doesn't, I do."

"Okie dokie then. I can buy that from you, too."

✝ ♥ ♫♪ •*•♪♫ ✝

Mercy, she had it all figured out. Samuel let her prattle on, making plans on top of plans, but the subject he wanted to broach, he couldn't get out. Every time he thought he had an angle on exactly how to ask, he chickened out.

He'd kept telling himself that it wasn't the right time, but the Holy Spirit told him different.

He needed to just spit it on out. Hoped to do that on the trip to Paris, intended to, but there hadn't been a long enough break in the action, and passing the hospital meant the jaunt came fast to its end.

At Highway 37, the first Clarksville traffic light where, normally, she'd turn left to get on the loop, she barreled straight into town and of course, drove straight to the bank.

He introduced her, and for sure, they'd be happy to loan her money on her land, his cows, her next album, or whatever. Amazing how a bit of fame opened doors. She left with a stack of papers to fill out in triplicate.

Hated banks, hated the thought of them being able to come take his equipment, or worse, his land. He desired to be in debt to no man—or bank.

She tossed him her keys. "Want to drive? I'll start getting these filled out."

He did as she asked, and headed through town out to Farm-to-Market 412, but it pained him that she was doing this. If God gave her a vision though, if her willingness to buy his herd proved to be of the Lord, it would all work out.

Pleased him that she heard and knew God's voice, and her seeing a vision…nothing less than exciting.

But he needed to liquidate, sell it all, land, cattle, equipment, everything, even his trailer. He wasn't married to any of it, and she could buy all of it that she wanted.

Well, he would like to keep PawPaw's house, at least long enough to tear it down and use what materials he could on her place. Maybe whoever bought it would agree to let him have salvage rights. He could even put it in the contract.

Only on the second page when he got them back in the woods to her new old house's site, she gave him an imploring expression. "Can you get started without me? But holler if you need me, and I'll come running."

"Sure." He left her scribbling and returned to getting her home in its proper place. The more he thought on it, the better he liked it—selling everything. He'd be so free, and he could buy the whole building.

Surely he could live upstairs somewhere, build himself a little corner apartment. Would the city let him do that? Didn't really matter. There were rooms to rent.

The Lord told him to do it, what? An hour ago? Spoke to his heart like always.

He jacked the last corner down, then backed off and knelt down to eye level. Maybe only one more round, two at the most, and he'd have her resting on the new blocks.

Then it dawned on him. He hadn't picked up any tie downs. Mercy, Lord, how could he forget those? Boy, what a rotten deal. It would be twice or three times harder now with the house in place.

He dusted himself off and strolled to her car. "Hey, we need to go to town."

"Yeah? What for?"

She looked up from her forms. Seemed like they expected her to write a book. Speaking of which, maybe she should—write a story about all this, her coming back home after two decades.

It'd make a great story, picking right back up with being his best friend—the School for the Prophets, and choir, and the new songs? It'd make a good book. Might even be fun to write it together.

"Hello? Earth to Samuel."

He gave her his attention.

"Why do we need to go to town? We were just there."

"I forgot the tie downs."

"What are they?"

"Big metal screws that I need to twist into the ground then attach the house to them with wire cables."

A blank stare, reconnection, then her face turned into a big question. "And why do we need them?"

"So that your house won't fly away." He pointed toward the sky. Dark clouds gathered, threatening the sunshine and challenging the blue sky. "Wind can blow right smart in these parts."

The air smelled of the coming rain.

"Aaaah, no tornado is going to blow my house down. Don't you know I have authority over the winds?" She grinned. "But if you want big screws, who am I to deny you? My car or do we need to take your truck?"

"Best take my truck. They're better than four feet long."

"Wow, I've never seen one that big." She glanced down at her papers. "Do you really need me? I'd like to finish the application."

"Guess not, but I'd just as soon you not fill them out."

"Why not? You don't want to sell me your cattle?"

He knelt to where he could see her face better. "I've decided to sell it all, not just the stock, but the land and equipment, too. I heard the Word of the Lord, and He said it was time to start the school.

"He's been telling me about it ever since I got saved, and I believe you were the key. Now that He's brought you back to me, then... Well, it's time to be about it, and we sure don't need any debt hanging around our necks."

She waved him back. He stood and retreated a few steps. She got out. "Now listen to me, Baylor, your PawPaw worked hard to

get that land. It's your inheritance. You can't sell it. He'd turn over
in his grave if you did any such thing."

"No, he wouldn't. My inheritance from him is way more than
some dirt. He taught me so much, but best of all, he lived a Godly
life before me, gave me a great example, and kept the faith to the
bitter end. That ranch and those cows are worth nothing compared
to being obedient to the Lord."

"What if you're wrong?"

"I'm not, I know I'm not. Think of that song He just gave us.
The same song at the same time, and mercy, girl, how many lives
is it going to change?"

"I'm sorry, you're right. But I saw your cows, I knew they
were yours, in my bottoms. So what do you make of that? And
selling your land just hurts my heart. Please let me do this.
Borrowing money makes so much more sense than selling your
stock, especially now that they're paying for their own way, plus
profit."

"We'd be tied to Clarksville. Always having to get home to
feed. What if the Lord wanted us to go…." He shrugged. "To
darkest Africa? Or somewhere really scary like Austin?"

"Right."

He grinned. "You have no idea how hard it is to get someone
to care for your animals like you do."

She held her hands up. "Okay, an hour ago you accused me of
rushing in where angels fear to tread."

"I didn't exactly phrase anything that way. What are you
talking about?"

She smirked. "Whatever. Anyway, who's going off the deep
end now? Wanting to sell out everything?"

"What happened to being all in? By the way, lock stock and
barrel is an old flintlock term, but it means the whole nine yards."

"I suppose you know what that means, too?"

He laughed. Nine yards? Of course I do, want to hear it?"

"No, that's really not what I want to know at all. Samuel Levi
Baylor, do you still love me?"

He nodded.

"What was that? Sorry, I didn't hear you."

He filled his lungs. This was it. Was he going to lose her now? "Yes, Mary Esther, I do love you with my whole heart. More than life. I always have, and I know…I always will."

A ray of sunshine broke through the trees. She stepped toward him, into heaven's spotlight.

"Okay. That's good. I really like that answer because I love you the very same way. I told you so at the studio. But then you wouldn't commit, and I couldn't figure out why. What's wrong? I just don't get it."

"I didn't mean…."

"So what are we going to do about our love?"

He shook his head and exhaled a heavy sigh. "I don't know what to do."

"Well, I do, you big dummy. Ask me to marry you."

Tears welled in his eyes then overflowed. He gasped. "Oh Lord, I… I…can't."

"You can't? Why in the world not, Samuel? You're in charge of you! Can't or won't?"

He ducked his head. How could he look at her? How could he break her heart? But he had to obey God, and He'd clearly laid out the criteria that had actually been a protection all these years. A means to keep him from temptation. "You…."

"Just forget it." Her hand slipped into his and tugged. "Come on. We're going to Colorado."

He let her pull him toward her car a step then stopped and found his voice. "Why Colorado?"

"Because! That's where mother and Ralph are. We'll fast and pray or whatever it takes to get him right."

"Ralph? He doesn't matter. It's you. You're not…."

"Not what? For goodness sake, I'm looking right at you and no cat has got your tongue!"

"Being a…." How could he? If only he'd never….

"What's so hard to say? Spit it out, Baylor."

"You not being a virgin." There. It was out, and now she would hate him and leave again.

Oh, God, Father God. Why did You ever bring her back to me? Only to lose her again? I can't stand it. If she goes again...I can't believe You meant to rip my heart out like this.

She recoiled like he'd just slapped her. "What? Who says I'm not? Who have you been talking to, because I never –"

"Well...uh...the other day...uh."

"What? You can preach to a whole room of strangers, but you can't talk to the girl you say you love more than life? Who told you I wasn't a virgin?"

"The other day, when I explained who I'd marry, stated the criteria between the Lord and me, I...I...Why didn't you say something?"

"Well, I did, you big dummy. Right after you said that, I told you about Ralph. Remember? How he'd tricked us. I thought all this was about him, and that it wasn't fair at all since he was not the man who raised me. By the way, it's just wrong to judge me unfit because of a man I'd hardly ever lived with."

"Wait. You thought I was talking –"

"Of course, I thought that you were talking about him! Samuel, I have never been with another man. And only for God's sake! To honor Him. I promised to save myself, but I never knew who I was saving that gift for. Almost as soon as I got back, I knew without a doubt. It's you. Of course, I'm a virgin, goof."

The weight that had held him down suddenly lifted and if he hadn't known better, he'd think he might float. "Oh, Mary Esther, so am I, my love."

"Really? You are? I wouldn't have figured –"

His finger touched her lips.

He knelt onto one knee and took her hand.

Someway, somehow, the Lord worked everything out. The path to his first and only love stretched out before him clear of obstacles. His heart welled with love and gratitude to the Almighty Creator.

"Mary Esther Robbins, I have loved you true since that first day. I adore you and have never loved another."

The birds started singing in all the trees around them. Had they been there before? Little rays of sunshine shone down everywhere, glittering the ground. "Precious lady, sent from God, created to complete me, will you marry me? Be mine. Say you'll be my wife, and make me the happiest man alive."

She stared into his eyes, and he drank her in.

"Yes, oh yes,love. There's nothing—no thing—I'd rather do!"

He stood, and she flung herself into his opened arms. He swung her around and around and a roll of thunder gently rumbled overhead as though all of Heaven approved.

✝♥♫♪ •*•♪♫✝ *The End* ✝♥♫♪ •*•♪♫✝

Samuel and Mary Ester were joined in holy matrimony as quickly as possible. Her mother and Ralph flew in to help with arrangements. She kept saying they'd practically waited their whole lives for each other and what was a few more days, much to both of the lovebirds' chagrin.

Twinkling lights set off the lovely evening ceremony under a canopy raised on the town square with the whole town in attendance. Mary Esther sang a new song to him, *I Couldn't love You More,* and both recited their own vows.

To settle the matter of Samuel selling his land, the newlyweds decided to cast lots. If she drew the white rock, they'd kept the ranch, if the black, put it on the market. She noticed relief in his eyes when she opened her hand with the pristine white pebble resting on her palm.

They kept his cows, too, and with the fat check Brad's accountant sent her, they had exactly what they needed to buy the old furniture store on the square for the school.

God's provision never failed!

Upon closing her bank account, she still had plenty of bucks to finish the house. Samuel saved over eighty percent of his PawPaw's porch material, and used some of the more interesting roof boards to trim out one of the living room walls.

The School of the Prophets and the Lord's Choir at Clarksville opened on the same day, with seven singers and seven sons of the prophets in attendance, counting Sam and Mary.

But they didn't despise the small beginning. That's another story which can't be told until the fullness of time.

Five Star Reviews of
The Preacher's Faith...

Great story! Hope there's a sequel, and I'd love to see the artful dodger as a part of it. Maybe a reunion? And he could find his mother. Just love curling up in an afghan with a cup of cappuccino and reading Caryl's books! Keep on writing!
    --Lenda Selph, reader, New Boston, Texas

As with all Caryl McAdoo's novels, the book is full of good scriptural advice. The title is a play on words...does 'faith' refer to a personal faith or the person Faith or both? The Preacher's Faith is a quick and easy read, and just right for a cold winter's day - your heart will be warmed by this delightful little story.
    --Julia Wilson, reader, England, United Kingdom

This was my first book to read by Caryl McAdoo and I absolutely loved it. I will be reading more. I love the way she prays that her story gives God Glory and dedicates The Preacher's Faith to Him and His Kingdom...a good clean book to read. I was drawn into this story right from the start. I loved this book and can't wait for book two.
    --Elizabeth 'Liz' Dent, reader, Decatur, Alabama

Caryl McAdoo is a great storyteller and I was immediately drawn into this story. The characters were great and I loved the storyline. It had me turning the pages wondering is things were going to work out between Asa and Faith. I would definitely recommend this book.
    --Susan Johnson, reader, Odessa, Texas

I loved The Preacher's Faith! This has to be one of my favorites, and I hope to read more like it! Way to go, Caryl! Your stories always captivate me.
    --Leah Jones, reader, Morrow, Arkansas

The Preacher's Faith

A contemporary Christian Texas Romance / ISBN 978-0-6159-9574-8 / ASIN B00SJH7EU0

Can the orphaned preacher and the heartbroken rodeo queen navigate the path to true love with a lie and an ex-beau blocking their way?

Learning of Faith Johnson's rash promise to her father, New Hope Baptist's interim preacher Asa Davidson shows up to apply for the position—of husband. The cowgirl was only trying to give her dying father hope promising to marry the first thirty-something-year-old Christian virgin to ask. Who'd ever dream one existed in all of Texas, much less Red River County? But sure enough, one comes a'courting the very next day thanks to the Lord and Daddy's baby sister, loud mouth Aunt Iris. Faith's appalled, but a promise is a promise. She only needs to figure a way out.

Originally, Asa sees matrimony as a career move. He hopes a godly, local wife will seal the deal for a permanent call. Then asked right out about that very thing, he lies. Sparks fly when her past love and the preacher meet up, but as the days pass, she finds herself admiring the man and his relationship to God more and more. He's a hard worker and wonderful, fun companion. Maybe she could learn to love him. But what if New Hope doesn't call him? She loves it right where she's at. Plus what about her dying father? And there's that untruth between them....

And to make things even harder, her ex comes to Christ through it all!

Five Star Reviews of Book One
Vow Unbroken

With an intriguing plot line and well-developed characters, McAdoo, who's written nonfiction and children's fiction, delivers an engaging read for her first adult historical romance.
--*Publishers Weekly*

After reading Caryl McAdoo's story of Henry and Susannah in "VOW UNBROKEN," I felt like I'd had another adventure with Tom Sawyer and Becky, this time as young adults.
--Alan Daugherty: columnist *The News-Banner*

Caryl McAdoo is a new unique voice in historical Christian fiction. I fell in love with the characters from the very first page. They pulled me into their lives and kept me there through the whole interesting storyline. I found the setting authentic, and Caryl kept me turning pages. I know you'll love this book as well as I did.
--Lena Nelson Dooley, award winning, best-selling author of *Maggie's Journey, Mary's Blessing, Catherine's Pursuit* & many more novels

Loved this story! Fresh strong voice from Caryl McAdoo…most memorable character [heroine Sue Baylor] I've encountered in some time. Well plotted and nicely paced. There's a Louis L'Amour and All-American feel to Caryl's writing. Beautiful romance, one of the nicest I've seen in a while.
--Carrie Fancett Pagels, author of *Return to Shirley Plantation*, a Civil War romance

Historicals by Caryl McAdoo

Vow Unbroken

A historical Christian Texas Romance from Howard Books, Simon & Schuster division; Book One / ISBN 978-1-4767-3551-1 / ASIN B00DPM7UYY

Susannah Baylor reluctantly hires Henry Buckmeyer in 1832 to help her along the Jefferson Trace, the hard stretch of land between her Northeast Texas farm and the cotton market, where she's determined to get a fair price for her crop. It's been a long, rough ten years and the widow's in danger of losing the land her husband and his brother left to her and the children, and she needs help to get both her wagons safely to Jefferson.

She knows Henry's reputation as a lay-about and is prepared for his insolence, but she never expects his good looks or irresistible, gentle manner. Soon they are entwined in a romantic relationship that only gets more complicated because Henry doesn't know God the way she does. Dangers arise on the trace—but none as difficult as the trial her heart is going through. Will Susannah and Henry's love overcome their differences?

And will she get her crop to market and sell it for enough to save her farm? In this heartening and adventurous tale, a young woman's fortitude, faith, and heart are put to the ultimate test.

Five Star Reviews of Book Two
Hearts Stolen

Christian Romantic Historical Western Adventure Fiction-- a BIG genre for a whole lot of novel. For me, McAdoo vaulted immediately into the ranks of a great writer I'll follow closely.
-- Howard "Doc" Wolfe, top Amazon reviewer

Caryl McAdoo is an entertaining storyteller! *Hearts Stolen* kept me up late, turning page after page, with an eagerness to know how the love story would end. I enjoyed this emotional journey of love and loss and look forward to continuing the trilogy in *Hope Reborn*!
--Britney Adams, reader, Texas

A great novel. I loved the characters, setting, history, and plot. I found the storyline quite unique. Just when I thought I knew how it will end, there was an unexpected twist. Highly recommended! 5 stars!
--Amy Campbell, reader, Salem, Virginia

Get ready for a wild, uplifting, heart-tugging, page-turning ride. *Hearts Stolen* grabbed me at the start. Sassy's feisty, fighting spirit...I couldn't set it down. Burnt dinner, but forget eating, I ate this book up. Caryl's a master storyteller weaving Texas history into a well-crafted plot with unforgettable and totally loved characters.
--Holly Michael, author, *Crooked Lines*

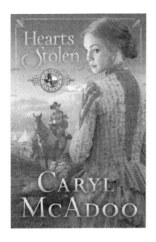

Hearts Stolen

A historical Christian Texas Romance;
Book Two / ISBN 978-1-5003-3651-6 /
ASIN B00NAXGAZI

Unbeknownst to loved ones, a headstrong young wife is snatched off the prairie by two Comanche braves, carried north of the Red River, and traded to their war chief for ponies. After five years, a small detail of Texas Rangers rides into camp, and she determines that day will bring freedom or death. She'll remain captive no more.

Sassy Nightengale almost gives up hope until that company of rangers rides into Bold Eagle's peace camp. They've come for the negotiated exchange of stolen whites, except neither her name nor her son's is on their list.

Famed Texas Ranger Levi Baylor spots the red-headed beauty and agrees to the war chief's high price, adding his personal horse and favorite weapon to the Republic's agents' offerings. The trade propels the couple on a trail of joy and sorrow.

Sweet love blossoms but must be denied. His integrity and her faith in God keep them at arm's length, not even allowing a kiss. Sassy's still married to her son's father, and Levi's honor-bound to deliver her home—to her husband.

Can their forbidden love be made holy? God hates divorce. Will Nightengale relinquish his wife and son? Will Sassy and Levi find the redemption they search for their troubled souls?

Five Star Reviews of Book Three
Hope Reborn

I loved the characters in this book, and I thought it was so much fun that Ms. McAdoo put her novels in as though they were written by May. This was a great story and I can't wait until the next one comes out.
    –Susan Johnson, reader, Odessa, Texas

I waited eagerly for this book and definitely wasn't disappointed! Caryl once again authored a beautifully written story with well developed characters. Wonderful addition to the series!
    --Amber Merchant, reader, Irving, Texas

Ms. McAdoo once again gripped me from page one. (read almost one sitting.) These Texas Romances, Christian Historical Western Adventures, are certainly full of all of the aspects of each genre individually meshed into a wonderful, very unique, unforgettable story.   --Rachelle Williams, reader, Mississippi

With memorable characters, Caryl's signature humor, and plenty of adventure, drama, and romance, "Hope Reborn" is anything but fluff. A strong message of salvation runs through, but well within the storyline. Enjoyed a unique twist with May writing the stories of the previous characters – clever and fun!
    --Pam Morrison, reader, Mason, Tennessee

I loved it. A real Christian story. I love Caryl's books because they are exciting, funny and with a lot of love and respect. Many great characters and great dialogues. Never boring.
I can't wait to read the next book. Great job Caryl McAdoo.
    --Catherine Peterson, reader, Denmark

Hope Reborn

A historical Christian Texas Romance;
Book Three / ISBN 978-1502-8170-4-4
/ ASIN B00RASZWEY

New York novelist May Meriwether
decides a heroic Texas Ranger will
make a great love interest for her new novel's heroine. Bored
to tears and loving adventure—keeps her mind off her
solitude—she sets out to the Lone Star State with her constant
companion and confidant Chester in tow.

Dreams for a husband and children are relegated to the
recesses of her heart; the self-confessed old maid deems it's too
late. But the near-perfect widower resurrects a smidgeon of
hope.

Only his impenetrable, superstitious religious beliefs stand
in the path to her falling head over heels, those and his love for
his dead wife. Would there ever be room for her in his heart?

And would he give up his fanaticism over God?

An unexpected romance surprises both. Hope is reborn in
God's unfailing love and grace. Can a life built on lies find the
Way to confession, forgiveness, and true joy? In a day when
the church offers the only stability on the 1850 Texas prairie,
these unlikely players find one another and fall in love.

But will it be enough?

Five Star Reviews of Book One
Lady Luck's a Loser

I really enjoyed this book. Couldn't put it down. I loved that the characters are more mature and not entirely perfect If you are a more mature reader, as I am, and would like to read about more mature characters I recommend this book. Younger readers would it enjoy it too!

--JoAnn Stewart, reader, Defuniak Springs, Florida

I really like this book! I love plots that are different, not the same old regular love story. I enjoyed that the characters were not the "normal" that they were older and not your skinny beautiful people. I loved that the story kept my attention the entire way.

--Teresa Denise Summers, reader, Irving, Texas

A very unique, witty plot. I couldn't put it down. I love that my favorite charactors are still very much active at the end of the book only their relationships have changed. What a way for Dub to fulfill his promises to his deceased wife. Love, trust, forgiveness, and many emotions make for a well written book.

--Joy Gibson, reader, Oneida, Tennessee

Lady Luck's is a Loser is such a fun and quick read. The storyline is unique and clean. The characters are interesting and believable. I love the setting too. If you are looking for a good, clean, quick, and romantic story, then this book is for you. A definite page turner.

--Amy Campbell, reader, Salem, Virginia

Apple Orchard Romance

Lady Luck's a Loser

A contemporary mature
inspirational romance; Book 1, an
Apple Orchard Romance / ISBN 978-
0-6159-9574-8 / ebook ASIN
B00JCC5YI0

Marge Winters answers the ad for
manager at a Bed & Breakfast, placed
by a wealthy widower seeking a new wife. W. G. Preston,
avoids the dating game by hiring eight diverse women to live at
his B&B--to be themselves while he gets to know them.

It's soon apparent he can't take six months with all eight
and devises a plan to eliminate one per month, leaving the
decision to Lady Luck, as he successfully has so many times.

The women compete to win his wedding ring. The widow
grandmother Marge is witty and friendly, yet naive. Youngest,
Vicki hides her enchanting vulnerability with a queenly
persona. Audrey, a great listener and cook, can be quite moody.
The cute Natalie has trouble making friends.

Beautiful Virginia harbors a secret, and energetic Holly
lifts everyone's spirits, but ruins her wholesome image.
Charlotte loves antiques, as did the first Misses Preston, and
Dorothy is quite a leader, but Preston isn't looking for a
manager. He wants a wife.

Lady Luck's a Loser is an amusing character study that
hooks readers through the depth provided to the cast, which
enables the novel to avoid the pitfalls of *How to Marry a
Millionaire* and *The Bachelor*. A difficult accomplishment,
each of the key players can be distinguished from one another.

Five Star Reviews of Volume One of The Generations

A Little Lower Than the Angels

The best way to enjoy a book or your Bible, is to put yourself in it…see, feel, smell, and touch, be sure you experience…the emotions they feel; anger, love, hate, betrayal, sadness and happiness-just what Christians today deal with. How wonderful that God is loving and forgiving as we often are tempted and go astray and Caryl brings this to light with her characters.

--Michelle Rhoden, reader, Paducah, Kentucky

Adam and Eve tempted. Seduced by evil, Cain kills Abel. Caryl McAdoo gives her spin on this captivating story in Genesis. I did enjoy reading the story of Eve's betrayal, Angels and the Wonders of Heaven, the pain of Adam and Eve losing their children. Caryl gives biblical scripture and insight to this story at the end of the book. You can look up and read the scriptures she refers to throughout this book. I recommend this book.

--Deanna Stevens, reader, Beatrice, Nebraska

Caryl McAdoo used her research and knowledge of biblical scripture combined with an incredible imagination as a foundation to fill in the gaps of the story of Adam and Eve and their children. I was caught up in the story from page one to the ending. I particularly appreciated the "Search the Scriptures" section at the end which explains some of the Biblical clues that guided this work of fiction. I loved "A Little Lower Than the Angels" and highly recommend it.

--Judy Levine, reader, Prescott, Arizona

A Little Lower Than the Angels

A Biblical fiction; Volume One of The Generations series ISBN 978-1502412270 / ebook ASIN B00P4UXEU4

Running three parallel storylines, *A Little Lower Than the Angels* opens with the sacrifices offered to God by Adam and his two sons Cain and Abel. Everyone knows the story, but this novel brings it to life from a new perspective.

One story follows Cain after the murder. He flees Adam's Valley with his sister Sheriah traveling to Nod, east of Eden. Marked and cursed as a vagabond, he becomes easy prey for Satan and his minions, ever moving further and further from the teachings of his father and obedience to God. (Scripture says he went to Nod with his wife, and that Eve is the mother of all the living, so she must be the mother of the woman Cain takes as his wife, making her his sister as well.)

Another tells of Abel's adventures in Paradise. He enters in at the death of his earthly flesh. Father God sends the first of the cherubim, a wonderful character named Namrel, to greet him and teach him, help him adjust to his new home. Abel meets his parents' Garden of Eden pets, Lion and Lamb, and Centurion, a large angel of the host. He learns how earthly prayers loose the angels to war on earth's inhabitants' behalf—and how they fight.

Lastly, we remain in Adam's Valley and mourn with the bereaved parents, facing the loss of their three children. He and Eve relive different times in their lives as God helps them to endure and brings them to repentance.

Five Star Reviews of Volume One of
The Generations
Then the Deluge Comes

Beautifully written, the novel concentrates on Noah leading up to the flood. Caryl McAdoo takes nothing away but enhances the biblical story. The characters are fully developed, becoming more three dimensional than in the Bible. And not only does the reader see the earthly version, but glimpses of the heavenly one, too. There is so much beauty in Caryl McAdoo's retelling of the traditional story, the reader just revels in the language. Then The Deluge Comes is a quick read, just right for an afternoon or an evening. It will leave you feeling calm and peaceful, and you will be glad that you picked it up.
--Julia Wilson, teacher and reader, United Kingdom

Deluge is the second book in The Generations Series, and if the books still to follow are as good as this one and the first one in the series are it is going to be an incredible series. The author has a way of breathing life and emotions into the characters that made me feel like I was on the sidelines watching their stories unfold. This is some of the best Biblical fiction that I have read and I look forward to the rest of the series. I was furnished with an e-copy of the book in return for an honest review.
--Ann Ellis, reader, Texas

Then the Deluge Comes brings Enoch, Methuselah, Lamech, and Noah to life. When Enoch is taken up, he visits with an ancient angel. These insights bring depth to the biblical story. I feel like I am there as they are getting the ark ready.
Reading about Noah's mother, sons, and where their wives came from opened up their lives. Caryl McAdoo's story brings God's to life. My favorite part, Search the Scriptures, tells how the Bible backs up her fictional story. She relates scripture after scripture, like a mini Bible lesson. I look forward to many more books by this author. For an encouraging, uplifting, and eye-opening read, I recommend Then the Deluge Comes
--Sally Shupe, reader, Virginia

Then the Deluge Comes

A Biblical fiction; Volume Two of The Generations series ISBN 978-1503197459 / ebook ASIN / March 6, 2015

Obedience assures the preservation of life. By Adam's death, evil rules the sons of Cain who fill the earth with their lasciviousness and violence. God declares He will not contend forever with man. But, Noah, the only one of the tenth generation to walk perfectly before the Lord, hears His Word.

MAKE THEE AN ARK OF GOPHER WOOD ROOMS SHALT THOU MAKE IN THE ARK, AND SHALT PITCH IT WITHIN AND WITHOUT WITH PITCH

With the help of his father Lamech, and Grandfather Methuselah whose name foretells when the deluge will come, Noah and his three sons embark on the massive task of building the giant boat with no idea why except that God said to. As the vessel of their salvation nears completion, it becomes apparent Noah's sons need wives, but their mother left off childbearing before birthing any daughters.

Evil, too, heard the Word of the Lord, and Lucifer and his angels war in the Heavens to destroy the earth's inhabitants. With each child that is passed through the fire, their battle songs grow stronger.

Lamech journeys to the land of Nod to find suitable maidens for his three grandsons, but can he find anyone pure enough there? And where in all the world and Heaven is the Almighty to get enough water to float the ark, much less cover the face of the earth?

And Coming Soon…

Sins of the Mothers in May!

A historical Christian Texas Romance; Book Four / **May 3, 2015**, God willing / ISBN 978-1503197541 / ebook AISN

True love mends what blind love has broken.

At much too tender an age, manipulated by her love for the older and handsome Caleb Wheeler, Mary Rachael defies her father, takes her inheritance, and sneaks off in the dark of morning to marry without her father's blessing.

She runs off to California to open a new business with her brand new husband and his cousin who's waiting there. Once she's far enough away that it's impossible for Mary Rachel's daddy to send anyone after her, she telegraphs him in care of a New York publisher.

Her step-mother offers to cancel their trip and her book tour in Europe to return to Texas and retrieve the wayward eighteen-year-old, but her father, the renowned Henry Buckmeyer knows the die is cast.

Already married, his firstborn has sown to the wind, and he can but pray she will not reap the whirlwind. However, that's exactly what the young bride encounters in the gold rush days of San Francisco.

After finding her husband is far from the man she thought he was, she's attracted to a successful business man who may even be worse. By a quirk, she's partnered with the one man who has the heart to redeem her, but he rubs her wrong at every turn.

Doomed to repeat the sins of her mother and grandmother, will Mary Rachel Buckmeyer Wheeler ever find her way back home and be reconciled with her daddy? Or is it too late?

One and Done ~ A contemporary Christian Texas Romance / **July, 2015**

Samantha Danielle gets the break she's dreamed of—being a sportscaster! George Herman Walter Johnson, Gij for short, is smitten, but the lady must get right with the Lord to win the Texas Ranger's oldest-ever rookie.

CHAPTER ONE TEASER BELOW! ☺

Token of the Covenant

A Biblical fiction; volume 3 of The Generations series / **August 8, 2015**

Noah & Hattimas, Japheth, Ham, and Shem work on the ark tending God's animals thinking anyone can stand forty days and forty nights. They hope Noah heard right and the rain would stop. Then they could return to living on dry ground, but they discover that's only the beginning of their time on the ark.

Daughters of the Heart

A historical Christian Texas Romance, Book Five / **September, 2015**

Gwendolyn, Cecelia, and Bonnie come of age and the young men come courting from all over the state, but after seeing how devastated their father was when Mary Rachel ran off, the sisters enter into a pact never to break his heart.

Acquiring a Wife ~ A contemporary Christian Texas romance / **October, 2015** / Ethan hires Jade to play a game of strategy and high finance as a ruse to see if his first impressions hold true and she's worthy of matrimony, but she proves no easy acquisition.

Children of Eber

A Biblical fiction; volume four of The Generations series /
November 2, 2015
Abraham, Sarah, Ishmael, and Isaac live out their stories.

SON OF MANY FATHERS

A historical Christian Texas Romance / Book Six / Jan. 2016
Charley Nightengale comes home from the Civil War to
find Lacey has run off, heading out to join the People of her
father and Charley takes out after her alone.

For your enjoyment… a preview of

Red River Romance ~ book four, a
contemporary Christian Romance coming July 2015

One and Done

Chapter One

"Hey. Weather girl."

Sammi Dan stopped in her tracks. Crackers, what did he want? With a million and two things to do, she sure didn't need any distractions this morning. She turned. Her boss stood at the end of the hall just outside his office waving a brown paper envelope in the air.

Mister Yancy had hardly said four words to her in the year she'd been with KBTL.

She stepped toward him. "Yes, sir? Is there a storm? Because if there is, I swear, I didn't hear a thing about it."

"You're the one with the guy's name, right?"

Oh, okay, here we go. "Yes, sir. Well, my parents named me Samantha Danielle, but most everyone calls me Sam. Or Sammi Dan."

He grinned. "I thought so. Joe says you like baseball. That right? You know some of the basics?"

So, he and the sportscaster had been talking about her. Could it be about the open slot in sports? She'd love that! Oooo, or maybe the company box? She'd remember to give the ex-quarterback a big thank you kiss if he'd put in a good word for her.

She added a touch of intentional pep to her tone. "Yes, sir. All my life." She closed the distance to a few feet, didn't want to seem too eager to get his Ranger tickets.

Hey, wait a minute. Though none of the other girls complained about the general manager getting fresh, Sammi Dan's guard hairs stood at attention. Just in case, she better say something. She certainly did not want any misunderstandings and found the best policy was always to be firm and honest right up front.

"Your passport up to date?"

Passport? She nodded as a tsunami slammed her backwards. No box seats, no sports position, not even a little harassment. There was a storm. Oh, bologna! She hated covering hurricanes.

"Yes, sir." She hadn't meant for that to sound so dejected.

He stuck out the envelope. "Take what's her name from the bullpen with you. This might be good. Joe caught wind of a rookie phenom the Rangers are hot after. He's pitching tomorrow night in Mexico City. Be there. Get ahead of this story."

She took the offering. "Yes, sir, whatever you say, sir. But why me? I'm the weather girl."

"I know who you are. Your numbers are trending." He backed toward his office. "You want to go or not?"

"Yes, of course. Very much so, sir. Thank you. I mean for thinking of me. Woo! I am plenty excited about this, I can tell you."

He didn't smile. What a geezer!

"There's a Visa in there." He pointed to the packet. "But best be wary of the sharks in accounting."

A company card! What a wonderful old, generous geezer. "Yes, sir. And thank you for your confidence in me. I'll not let you down, Mr. Yancy."

He waved her off like getting a shot at sports meant nothing and retreated to his office. Must be nice being general manger of DFW's biggest television station. She spun around then turned back.

What's her name in the bullpen? Okay, that left her choices wide open. Hmm, who'd be the most fun camera girl to fly south with? Or should she choose a guy? No, Yancy definitely said what's her name, so he indicated a female if little more.

Exactly six hours and forty-seven minutes later, Sammi Dan flopped down on one of the Hilton's double beds as though a kid again. Wow, she could hardly believe how fast it all happened. But there she was!

April 'what's-her-name' Meadows stood in front of the dresser and smirked unpacking her suitcase into the drawers. "Shouldn't we hurry up and get ready and go back downstairs? Aren't we running out of time?"

"Oh, girlfriend, lighten up for the sake of the team, will you? You're not being any fun." Sammi Dan pointed to the little refrigerator. "See what they've got to drink in there. And if there's any chocolate."

Her camera girl slash producer slash assistant shook her head. "You're unbelievable. I've already made arrangements for you to do a preliminary with this G. H. Johnson guy in exactly." She slid her phone open. "Fifty-two minutes in the lobby."

"Heavens to Mergatroid, girl, that's almost an hour away. Why the rush?"

"Yogi Bear? Really?" She shook her head as though disgusted. "Whatever. You're supposed to be the talent here, Sam. Don't you want to freshen up, get downstairs early for a lay of the lobby—choose the perfect shot for your interview? Or do you plan on lounging there sucking up the AC and drinking tequila with your chocolate truffles?"

Sammi Dan sat up and huffed. "It was Snagglepuss if you must know." Logical April was right of course, but she sure knew how to spoil a perfectly great trip to Mexico City. Should have asked Christie, she wouldn't be such a party popper.

Then again, her way with the camera didn't compare with April's. Sammi got up and riffled through her bag. The woman had an up close and personal relationship with great angles.

"I don't know why you're unpacking. What's the point when we're only spending one night? We do leave tomorrow after the game on the redeye, right? They could've let us fly home the next morning, but no, the sharks in accounting didn't want to spring for two nights."

G. H. Johnson showed early, but Sammi Dan had gotten there earlier. She loved that. Her chosen place for her first ever interview offered a lovely tropical backdrop of palm trees, ferns, and falling water.

She stood and stuck out her hand. "Good afternoon, Mister Johnson, and thank you so much for taking the time to meet with me. I'm Samantha Danielle Davenport from KBTL in Dallas. Won't you have a seat?"

"I know who you are."

He did? How in the world?

The man shook her hand with a firm grip, but didn't try to hurt her like some men who resented women in a man's field, then sat in the chair she'd indicated. "Why'd they send the weather girl?"

She looked at the towering ceiling and shook her head ever so slightly. Why, oh why? She'd hoped no one would be privy to that little tidbit of info.

"Apparently, I'm trending, and the word got out on how much I love baseball. Border on fanatic. Anyway, let's talk about you. Were you named after the Babe?"

"Yes and no." He pointed toward April. "Should she be taking some video?"

"Yes, of course. I mean if you don't mind. This is just a preliminary, but we might as well get some footage." She spun toward her camera gal. "Go ahead, we might want to splice some of this in." When the little red light on the camcorder glowed, she turned back to him. "I'll ask you again, okay?"

"Sure."

"So, Mister Johnson, were you –"

"Please, call me G. H."

She forced a smile. Why couldn't he just co-operate? "Alrighty then, good. Were you named after the great Babe Ruth, G. H.?"

"Yes and no. My full name is George Herman Walter Johnson. Pappaw wasn't sure what I was going to be, a slugger or a hurler."

"Your grandfather named you?"

"Yes, ma'am. Sure did."

"Well, my notes call you the next Walter Johnson. Says here the radar guns clocked you at over a hundred miles an hour." She pouted her bottom lip and shrugged. "Hate to bring up your somewhat rocky start, but after that, you're six-and-o in your last half-dozen games with an ought ERA. Care to comment?"

He didn't say anything for a minute.

She waited then glanced at April. Her red light still glowed. Sammi looked back to the pitcher.

He squinted. "Are your eyes always that green? Or are you wearing contacts? They don't come across so electric on the television."

Her face immediately heated, but she wouldn't let him get the best of her. No way. "Yes, that green. No contacts, ala' natural. And I don't know about the electric part, but yes they do look just like this on TV; you must not have high def. Now the comment I'm looking for, Mister Johnson, is on your last six starts. What happened?"

"Well, two things. I found the strike zone and a straight change."

"Are you excited about joining the Rangers?"

"Am I now?" He grinned. "Isn't a done deal yet. How old are you?"

This guy was incredible. What a flirt. And on camera, too.

He leaned forward and seemed to be checking her notes. "It's a fair question, you know my age." He pointed. "Right there, the year, month, and day."

She leaned away from him and glanced at April again and gave her can-you-believe-this-guy head shake and eye roll. But Sammi Dan's usual twenty-nine answer refused to pass her lips. For some reason, she didn't want to lie to this guy.

"That's a silly question. Why would you even want to know?"

"Just curious to see if I'm going to be breaking one of my rules or not."

Her face burned and her interview was out the window. She forgot all about the filming. "You have rules? Who do you think you are? Leroy Jethro Gibbs?"

"Ah, you like NCIS, too. I usually don't date older women, but in your case, I would make an exception. I've got to meet with my agent tonight, but what say we have dinner together after the game tomorrow?" He looked at April. "Want me to ask one of the hombres to join us?"

"Oh, no. I'll be fine. You two go ahead."

Sammi Dan gave his shoulder a little push, maybe more of a shove. "I'd love to. That'll be great, but I want April to come."

"Who's April?"

She turned off her camera and hung it at her side. "I am. Miss Davenport's producer, but I do not have to go—nor do I want to."

"Hey, I know y'all came for the interview, and you're welcome to shoot a quick one after the game." He looked to Sammi Dan. "I apologize for fooling around here, but four's a double date. Three's just a crowd."

"Excuse me, I hate to interrupt." A ditzy blonde tapped his shoulder then thrust her pad and pen at him. "I just have to have your autograph. You are The Deacon, aren't you?"

The Deacon?

He grinned again. He had an alluring almost-smile, nearly a smirk, but with a come-hither slant. "I was, but I don't play anymore."

"That's okay, I don't watch anymore. Not since you haven't been there." She pointed to the pad, repeatedly poking at it. "Sign it anyway for me, please. Make it out to Chrystal, that's C-H-R-Y-s-t-a-l. Starts off like the flower, you know, chrysanthemum, ends up the jewel. Mama did that to make me a special Chrystal. I just loved watching you play so much. What a game you've got."

The man signed the woman's paper, then the floozie in too-tight pants and ten inch streetwalker heels kissed his cheek and disappeared.

"So what was that all about?"

He shrugged. "Another time, another life. So are we on for dinner?"

Her face had cooled, and she rediscovered a mite of civility. "Okay, sure. Fine. I'll ditch the camera girl after our interview and eat with you as long as you take me somewhere expensive."

"Know just the place, a little tamale cart not too far, it's within walking distance. The proprietor wears a big hat, has a real classy burro named Latte, and serves the best tamales in town."

Sammi Dan scooted her chair back and stood. God's gift to humor this guy was not—but still cute—and besides, she'd never dated a phenomenon. She shook her head.

"No way, George. I was thinking someplace with a little more glitz and glamour. Don't you want to see me all dressed up?" She extended her hand, and he stood and took it. "So thank you again, Mister Johnson. Until tomorrow."

"What happened to G. H.?" He shook then kept hold of her hand. "Oh, and a word of warning, the Rojos are old school, no femalies in the locker room."

"Not a problem. Wouldn't want to go there anyway."

"If I finish what I start, I'll see you and April on the field for the official interrogation. Otherwise, how about we meet right here?"

She let him keep her hand. "Why not the stadium either way?" The contrast between his callused fingertips and the rest of his hand intrigued her.

"My agent seems to think I need a shutout to get the call we're waiting for."

She laughed. "Nothing like putting a little pressure on, is there?"

"I think that's the whole point."

Gij watched the weather girl walk away then thought on her all the way to his meeting. And she tuned up again in the TV in his head the next morning, too, almost as soon as he opened his eyes.

Maybe not beautiful, but highly attractive sure fit. Hard to believe the weather girl had shown up in Mexico City, of all the thousands of possibilities, tens of thousands. He allowed himself to think about Sammi Dan all the way to the ball park.

Once inside and dressed in his red pin striped uniform, he relegated her from his conscious and went to work on the pre-game reports. He had a shutout to throw. Between his little bit of Spanish and the Rojo's general manager's more decent English, he and the catcher got on the same page with every batter.

Then he found himself a quiet corner and went to his knees. For the longest, he waited, focused full on the Lord. Finally, a peace settled over then inside him.

"Thank You, Father. For Your glory and Your honor, find pleasure in me, Your creation. In Jesus' name, amen."

For seven innings, perfection. Then the first batter in the eighth leaned forward on an inside pitch and took it on the forearm. Wonder he didn't break his fool bone.

The next guy squared to bunt then slapped a dying quail to right field just over the charging first baseman's head.

Men on first and third. Great. Gij didn't need this.

The ball back in his glove, he stepped off the mound. "Well, old son, it's now or never." Nine heaters later, he strolled to the dugout. Their best hitter had only managed a foul, but his other eight tosses went untouched.

Three more outs, he walked off the Rojo's mound for what he hoped would be the last time. After fifteen minutes or so, when the fans started thinning, he met Samantha back out on the field as promised.

Her microphone crowded his mouth, and her camera girl's lights practically blinded him, but her unfettered enthusiasm charged him.

"I've never seen anything quite like it, G. H. Your whipsaw motion is just phenomenal. How'd you develop it?"

"Played third base in college, and it just came natural when I gave pitching a shot."

She pushed back the strand of hair that kept blowing across her face. "I watched the game sitting next to the Rangers' scout right behind home plate. Fastest you threw before the eighth was ninety-eight, but after the two guys got on base, the last nine went from a hundred and three all the way to a hundred six.

"How do you do it? Get faster instead of slower, I mean, seems it'd be the other way around."

"Best ask the Good Lord that one. I didn't make this arm."

The weather girl turned toward the camera. "Folks, I've never seen anything like it, and I've been watching baseball all my life.

"I can't see one reason why George Herman Walter Johnson shouldn't be pitching for the Rangers instead of the Rojo's. Really, Texas fans are in for a treat. I know I won't miss a game. This is Samantha Davenport reporting live from Mexico City."

She dragged her finger across her throat and faced him as the camera lights went off. "Instead of my usual beauty nap this afternoon, I Googled you. How do you suppose Major League Baseball is going to feel about a professional poker player in their ranks?"

"I do believe your eyes are even greener under the camera lights. You ever seen 'em in light that bright?"

"Duh, I have a makeup mirror. Why are you dodging my question? I didn't ask you when she was filming, so what's the deal?"

"I wasn't doing anything illegal. And I have never bet on a baseball game, not ever. Actually, I'm not even a gambler. I used to be a poker player, and now I'm a baseball player."

"Simple as that." Just like a female, she wanted more than he was willing to give.

"Isn't it?"

"Okay then, why did the University of Texas kick you out of Longhorn baseball right before the College World Series?"

"They didn't. I flunked out. Spent too much time at the hold 'em tables."

"I see said the blind man." She batted her lashes. "So where are you taking me for dinner? And can you even wait to get back to Texas our Texas?"

"All hail the mighty state." He grinned. "I am looking forward to that. Playing for the Rangers... Wow."

"I'm sayin'."

Reach out to the author...

Website   http://www.CarylMcAdoo.com

Newsletter http://tinyurl.com/TheCaryler
            (Get FREE books for subscribing!)

Reviewers   http://carylmcadoo.com/christian-evaluaters
            (Join Caryl's Street Team!)

Blog   http://www.CarylMcAdoo.blogspot.com

Facebook   www.facebook.com/CarylMcAdoo.author

Twitter   http://www.twitter.com/CarylMcAdoo

G'Reads   http://tinyurl.com/GoodReadsCaryl

Google+   http://tinyurl.com/CarylsGooglePlus

Pinterest   http://www.pinterest.com/CarylMcAdoo

LinkedIn   www.linkedIn.com/CarylMcAdoo

Author Pages :
Amazon   http://tinyurl.com/CarylsAmazonAuthorPage

Simon & Schuster http://tinyurl.com/S-SCarylsPage

Email   ComeVisit@CarylMcadoo.com

Praying my story gives God glory! ☺
Blessings, Caryl

Author reaching out to you!

Hey dear Reader!

Where would I be if not for you? I always pray my story gives God glory and hope you enjoyed it. My desire is that it brought you closer to Him and gave you issues to ponder, asking for God's perspective.

If you'd like to stay right on top of all my book news, I'd love you to subscribe to my email newsletter The Caryler which comes each month to your Inbox. I try to make it fun with a Scripture of the day and a lyric of the day. God gives me new songs—a few introduced in this book—and there's nothing I'd rather do than praise and worship Him in song!

I include a few of my favorite things in it, too. My husband, being my favorite man, has a little corner and shares a few of his thoughts. I include other Christian authors and bloggers, sometimes a movie or book review, or a song.

What I'm working on, what's finished and coming out soon, and sales coming up on different titles. And the best part—as far as you're concerned—is that as my thank you for being a subscriber and following me, I'll give you a FREE e'BOOK every quarter! Four new books a year! Who can beat that? You can sign up at my website www.CarylMcAdoo.com in the right column on my Home page.

I hope if you like my story, you'll take the time to review it and click "follow" under my picture while you're there. ☺ And of course that you'll tell your friends. I love visiting with my readers, and have a group of special readers who help me spread the word when I have a new release. Let me know if you'd like to be a part of the Christian eVALUaters. Stop by my Facebook page, too!

Always out of room before I'm through visiting!

Love in Christ and many blessings,

Caryl

A few of Caryl's New Songs

Your Will

I just want to be in Your Will, Father
I just need to know Your Will.

I just want to be in Your Will, Father
I just need to know Your Will.

For to walk in obedience
is what I want to do.
For to walk in obedience
shows how much I love You.

Open my ears, Lord; so I can hear.
Help me to listen as I draw near.
Silence my flesh, Lord, in Jesus' name,
And by the power of His blood, I will proclaim
That demons and devils will not speak to me.
I'll not hear their lies or their blasphemies.
I only will hear
the clear voice of my Lord,
And then I'll obey
Your every Word.

I just want to be in Your Will, Father
I just need to know Your Will.

Choose

Choose, My child, you have a choice!
Choose whom you will serve this day!
Choose my child then lift up your voice!
Either blessings or curses are on the way!

Chorus
Choose Life – not death!
Choose love – not hate!
Choose liberty – not chains!
Choose My child to obey!
Choose who in your heart will reign!

Choose, My child, which path you'll take
Choose the wide or the narrow way!
Choose Heaven o'er the fiery lake
Favor will come when you obey!   *Chorus*

Choose, My child, the choice is yours
Guard the Truth or tell a lie
Your choice will open up the doors
Walk into abundance or barely get by!   *Chorus*

Choose My child, what matters most
My patience and joy, My promises receive!
Choose Satan's fruit or My Holy Ghost's
It's how you act shows what you believe. *Chorus*

Choose, My child, the words you speak
For I will create the fruit of your lips
Your words get to your future ahead of you
What you said yesterday, you're now walking through!   *Chorus*

Choose, My child, in whom you'll put your trust
Only death comes through your flesh man
My time is perfect, and My cause just
Whenever you need help, My Spirit can!   *Chorus*

Continued...

Choose, My child, choose humility
Pride always goes before a fall
Don't puff out your chest, boast, are brag on yourself
Then I'll lift you high to answer My call.   *Chorus*

Choose, My child, not to complain
Instead, Rejoice! in me and give praise
My Hebrew people wandered forty years
On a trip should've taken eleven days!   *Chorus*

Choose to love your enemy
It's easy to love a friend
Love always covers, sets captives free
Love never fails – It's good to the end.   *Chorus*

The Blood of Christ

The blood of Christ declares I am healed
By this precious Blood, love is revealed.
His shed red blood, it cleanses me.
The Blood of Yeshua bought my liberty.
      It's not the blood of goat or ram;
      It's the Blood of the Great I Am!
      It's not the Blood from a mere man,
      Praise God for His Blood that CAN - - -
            Wash away sin's stain, make me white as snow
         Give me power to walk in the way I need to go.
         It gives me strength to stand from day to day
         His redeeming Blood points me to The Way!
(Chorus)
Oh the Blood, the Blood, God's precious Blood
It's full of power for this very hour!
Oh the Blood, the Blood defeats our enemies
Lets the whole world see that we've been set free
Oh the Blood, the Blood, our Covenant!
The life is in the Blood. His life is in the Blood.

The Blood of Christ declares my righteousness
His freely given Blood stirs my consciousness
Eternal life now belongs to me.
Hope beyond today, my victory!
I'm so blessed to be beneath its flow
It's the Blood that always bids me go
Forth and focus on its Holy benefits
Hallelujah for His Blood that LETS - - -
Me share His great love, go into all the world
For His Blood spans all time, from its beginning to end.
It's protected and kept me since my youth
His beautiful Blood leads me to <u>The Truth</u>!
(Chorus)

The Blood of Christ declares I'm justified,
Shed at Calvary, my Lord crucified.
The peace of God and with God is mine,
By the gift of His Blood, pure and divine.
It's not the blood on an alter spilled
It's the Blood of my Savior who no man killed
He freely gave His Blood, it removed all doubt.
Glory to Him! His Blood prompts me to SHOUT - - -
My life's stamped by the Blood, I am His property!
His blood brings experience of Heaven's glory.
It puts an end to all fear, turmoil, and strife.
The Blood of the Lamb guides me to <u>The Life</u>!

(Chorus)
(Last time through)– His life is in the Blood, The life is in His Blood

Made in the USA
Charleston, SC
16 April 2015